TERMINAL VELOCITY

www.andymcnab.co.uk
www.rbooks.co.uk

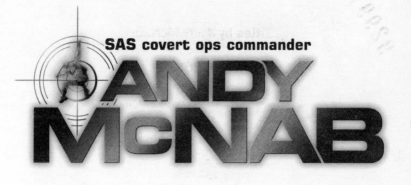

SAS covert ops commander

ANDY McNAB

DROP**ZONE**

TERMINAL VELOCITY

DOUBLEDAY

DROPZONE: TERMINAL VELOCITY
A DOUBLEDAY BOOK 978 0 385 61711 6
TRADE PAPERBACK 978 0 857 53004 2

Published in Great Britain by Doubleday,
an imprint of Random House Children's Books
A Random House Group Company

This edition published 2011

1 3 5 7 9 10 8 6 4 2

Copyright © Andy McNab, 2011

With thanks to David Gatward

The Random House Group Limited supports the Forest Stewardship
Council (FSC), the leading international forest certification organization.
All our titles that are printed on Greenpeace-approved FSC-certified paper
carry the FSC logo. Our paper procurement policy can be found at
www.rbooks.co.uk/environment.

Mixed Sources
Product group from well-managed
forests and other controlled sources
www.fsc.org Cert no. TT-COC-2139
© 1996 Forest Stewardship Council

Set in DIN

RANDOM HOUSE CHILDREN'S BOOKS
61–63 Uxbridge Road, London W5 5SA

www.kidsatrandomhouse.co.uk
www.rbooks.co.uk

Addresses for companies within The Random House Group Limited can be
found at: www.randomhouse.co.uk/offices.htm

THE RANDOM HOUSE GROUP Limited Reg. No. 954009

A CIP catalogue record for this book is available from the British Library.

Printed and bound in Great Britain by Clays Ltd, St Ives plc

GLOSSARY

AAD	Automatic Activation Device: senses rate of descent and altitude – mechanically activates reserve parachute if a skydiver passes below a set altitude at a high rate of descent.
A/C	Aircraft.
Accuracy	Also known as 'precision landing'. Competition discipline in which the skydiver tries to land on a target three centimetres in diameter.
AFF	Accelerated Freefall training, comprising freefall jumps of forty seconds or longer, accompanied by a qualified jumpmaster.
Airspeed	Speed of a flying object through the air.
AK-47/AK	Kalashnikov automatic rifle firing 7.62 rounds.
Altimeter	Device indicating altitude.
Altitude awareness	Process by which a skydiver regularly checks the ground and altimeter.
BASE jump	Jump made from a fixed object rather than from an aircraft. BASE is an acronym for Buildings, Antennae, Spans (bridges) and Earth (cliff).
Bergen	A backpack, or rucksack.
Body position	Freefall body posture.
Bounce	To land at unsurvivable speed. Also to frap, or go in.
Brakes	The brake lines of the canopy are synonymous with steering lines. Used together, they slow the parachute. Used independently, they result in a turn.
Break off	To cease formation skydiving by tracking away from the formation prior to deploying the canopy.
Burble	An area of turbulence which occurs behind an object going through the air.
Call	Time remaining until you are to board the aircraft or jump out of it.
Canopy	Another name for parachute.

Chat-net	A closed network which allows a group of people to chat at the same time using electronic communications devices.
Cover	False details used by covert operators to describe their personal history.
CQC	Close-quarter combat.
Cut away	To release the main parachute. Standard emergency procedure prior to deploying the reserve.
DLB	Acronym for dead letter box/dead letter drop.
Drogue	In a tandem jump, a drogue parachute is deployed shortly after exiting the aircraft to reduce the speed of descent. It is later used to deploy the main canopy.
Dropzone/DZ	Skydiving centre.
Fall rate	Speed at which a skydiver falls. Matching fall rate is essential to successful formation skydiving. This is done with jumpsuits, weights and body position.
Flare	To pull down the brakes of the canopy to slow it down, thus increasing the angle of attack and reducing the descent rate.
Freestyle	Acrobatic individual skydiving.
Formation	1) A freefall skydiving formation of more than one jumper. 2) A flight of more than one jump plane.
GPS	Global Positioning System.
Grippers	Handholds built onto formation skydiving jumpsuits to make the suits easier to hold onto.
HAHO	High altitude, high opening jump.
Harness/container	Webbing/fabric holding main and reserve canopies to the skydiver.
Heading	Direction in which the aircraft, skydiver or parachute is facing.
Hook knife	Small knife carried in jumpsuit or on rig to cut lines or webbing.
Jumpsuit	An overall designed for skydiving.
Krav Maga	Israeli hand-to-hand combat system.

Main	The primary canopy.
MI5	Military intelligence security service responsible for protecting the United Kingdom against threats to national security.
Pinzgauer	All-terrain four- and six-wheel drive military utility vehicle.
Reserve	Auxiliary parachute carried on every intentional parachute jump.
Regiment (The)	General term used to refer to the SAS.
RIBs	Rigid inflatable boats.
Ripcord	Deployment system on all reserves and most student parachutes. The ripcord is a piece of cable with a handle at one end and a pin at the other. When pulled, the pin comes out of the closing loop holding the container shut, and the pilot chute is released.
Rig	Slang for the entire canopy, including main and reserve canopies and the harness/container.
Rigger	Someone with a recognized qualification stating that they have successfully met the requirements to be a parachute rigger.
RPG	Rocket-propelled grenade launcher.
RV	Rendezvous.
Selection	Specific period of extended training where by soldiers who wish to join the UKSF (SAS and SBS) are required to pass three stages (endurance; jungle training; and escape and evasion and tactical questioning).
Steering lines	The lines that run from the steering toggles on the rear risers to the trailing edge of the canopy.
Steering toggles	Handles attached to the ends of the steering lines.
Stress positions	Interrogation technique whereby the human body is placed in various positions to put increased strain on muscle groups.
Swoop	1) To dive down to a formation or individual in freefall. 2) To aggressively approach the landing area in order to produce a long, flat flare and exciting landing.

Tandem	Two skydivers share a rig, one of whom is in a separate harness that attaches to the front of the other harness.
Terminal velocity	The speed at which drag matches gravity, resulting in a constant fall rate. Generally terminal velocity for formation skydiving is 120–135 mph.
Toggles	Handles on the steering lines.
Track	Body position that creates a high forward speed. Used to approach or depart from other skydivers in freefall.
UKSF	United Kingdom Special Forces. General term to cover SAS/SBS.
Wave off	Before deployment a skydiver makes a clearly defined arm motion to indicate to others nearby that he is about to open his canopy.
X-ray	Enemy combatant.

CHARACTERS

Ethan
Driven by a fierce determination to make something of his life, Ethan will push himself to the limit, face his fears head on and stand by his friends no matter what. Skydiving is just the opportunity he's been looking for, and he doesn't want to be simply good, he's out to be the best. Period.

Johnny
Quick with the witty comments and fast in the air, he's a living, breathing definition of 'adrenaline junkie'. But beneath the smart-arse persona lies a seriously capable operator who doesn't know the meaning of the word quit. His only problem is that he likes to go it alone, and that doesn't always work well with a team.

Kat
Pretty, athletic and impulsive, she loves being that rare thing among her peers – a girl who skydives. She does it because she knows she's good at it and because it makes her sexy as hell.

Luke
The one the rest of the team depend on to make sure everything is safe and sorted. He's quiet, methodical, and all about the detail. When it comes to skydiving, if Luke doesn't know it, it's not worth knowing.

Natalya
A serious girl with a mysterious past buried deep somewhere in eastern Europe. No one quite knows where she came from or how she ended up skydiving in the UK.

Sam
A world-class skydiver, skilled undercover operator and exceptional soldier, Sam is tough, serious and a natural leader. He has a long history with the SAS – having led operations across the globe – and he hasn't exactly retired. He's responsible for bringing the team together in the first place. His word is law. And he's someone you really don't want to cross.

Gabe

Sam's key contact at MI5, which is about all that Gabe would like any of the team knowing about him. In his mid-thirties, he's ambitious and single-minded, qualities which enabled him to pass Selection in his early twenties. He's rarely seen by the team, communicating only with Sam. However, when he does show up, it's as good a sign as anything that something is going down.

Skydiving

You jump from a plane at 12,000 feet, reach speeds of over 120 mph, then glide in under your canopy, gazing at the most amazing view of the earth you'll ever see. Adrenaline never tasted this good.

Warning: **dangerously addictive.**

BASE jumping

You don't jump from a plane, but from a fixed object closer to the ground. BASE stands for Building, Antenna, Span (bridge or arch), Earth. Unlike skydiving, a BASE jumper rarely reaches terminal velocity (120 mph).

Warning: **this is the closest you can get to falling to your death without dying.**

Prologue

The cage was hexagonal, five metres wide, the walls over two metres high. The rubber floor was wet and slick with blood and sweat. Both fighters had lost their footing more than once. Both had turned it to their advantage, landed blows, drawn blood.

They had been at it nonstop for all of seven minutes and twenty-four seconds. Twenty-five . . . twenty-six . . . twenty-seven . . . No way would they make it all the way to ten minutes. No one ever did. It wasn't long, but it was long enough.

No rules.

No referee.

Just survival.

Or death.

The darkness around the cage buzzed with the sound of a dozen cameras filming the fight, the encrypted images streamed via satellite to a small number of private screens around the world. To get access to this exclusive entertainment, just two things were required: the right amount of money, and the right contacts. The only information you were given was the time of the fight, the code to break the encryption and how much money you might win. Or lose.

How you came by the money, clean or dirty, was your business. And as far as the contacts were concerned, they weren't exactly the kind you'd meet in an average betting shop. But if you knew how to find them, then you also knew that double-crossing them was a bad idea. A very bad idea indeed.

Only a few miles away, in a lounge lit only by a roaring fire, a man sat in a black leather chair, his well-manicured hands playing with the gold rings he wore. Leaning against his leg was a black cane topped with a silver ball. The wall above the fire was hidden behind a huge flat-screen television, which cast electric colours into the room to spill across the carpet. The picture was so clear, so perfect, he could almost smell the perspiration of the fighters, reach out and touch the wire walls of the cage. And the best bit was only seconds away . . .

The man in the lounge was enjoying himself. He wasn't quite sure how much he'd put down: five, maybe six million. But the money wasn't important. He had plenty. Couldn't spend it quick enough. Which was why he had come up with this little game for others to play in the first place, wasn't it? A select few with billions in the bank and a thirst for the extreme.

It was winning that he enjoyed. That was what life was all about. Winning was everything. By any means necessary. As anyone who'd taken him on in his field of business knew all too well.

Not that any of them were still alive to talk about it.

Like a snake sliding across glass, a thin smile slipped across the man's face as he sat forward, leaned in towards the television; he didn't want to miss any of the final moments . . .

CLASSIFIED – TOP SECRET

OPERATION: RAIDERS

Aim: Recruit, train and develop a high-performance skydiving team of five young people for specialist covert operations work.

Progress: The following candidate has been successfully identified and recruited:

ETHAN BLAKE

Age: 17
Height: 1.8 metres

Physical Description:
Black hair, athletic build, no defining physical features/markings (scars, tattoos etc.)

Background:
Currently lives with parents and younger sister. Has a good relationship with mother and sister, though relationship with father is clearly strained. One year left in school: grades satisfactory, but struggles with academic work; generally succeeds through determination.

Operation(s):
Brought in on a mission to carry out a HAHO jump with the team to a target site and cause sufficient disruption, through the use of diversionary explosions, to aid the recovery of a hard disk containing top-secret government data. This mission was carried out with success and he executed his role well. He has continued

to demonstrate considerable drive and determination and a willingness to learn. Though impatient at times, and allowing his own feelings to cloud his judgement at others, he is now becoming an integral part of the team. Ethan's skydiving skills will soon be on a par with the best in the team.

Development:
It is imperative that, while building the team's skydiving skills and teamwork, we do not lose sight of the fact that the team as a whole must be trained up in other vital skills for their wider role. Current priorities are developing techniques for survival; escape and evasion; resisting interrogation; CQC and explosives.

Sam

Team Leader.

1

'Shit!'

Ethan was expecting the usual jolt from the canopy as it exploded with a loud *crack!* in the air above, taking him from 120 mph to 10 mph in less than ten seconds.

It didn't happen.

All he heard was material flapping in the air and he knew something had gone seriously wrong. It was nearly six months since he'd done his tandem skydive with Sam, then been put through his AFF. He was now a member of a skydiving team. And he knew canopy failures were rare. *Not rare enough though,* he thought.

Panic gripped him round the throat, tried to squeeze him to death. He could feel it tightening, cutting off his air, suffocating him. Seconds felt like hours. He knew if he didn't sort this out he was only moments away from a messy death.

Start sparking, Eth . . .

Ethan focused on his body position, tried to stay stable, but it was difficult with his canopy going insane above him. He looked up to check his steering lines. They were in a seriously messed-up state, twisted round each other in a nightmare tangle. They looked more like a burst ball of string attacked by a cat than the tidy lines of a skydiving rig. And above them, his main canopy was completely and utterly useless.

Ethan knew if he didn't do something, he'd hit dirt in less than thirty seconds. It'd be a bounce to write home about. Except that someone else would have to do the writing; at this height and speed no way in hell would he survive – he'd be making an Ethan-shaped hole in the fields below.

He tried to think clearly, but all he could see and hear was the canopy above his head doing about as much good as a deflated balloon. It was flapping and dancing in the air, like it was laughing at him, enjoying the idea that he'd be dead in seconds.

Ethan shook his head to try and clear his mind, help him deal with the serious situation he was in. It didn't work.

He looked back up, grabbed the steering toggles, tried to get the canopy back into shape. He flicked his legs to spin his body, yanked again, but nothing worked. He was sweating now, and his muscles were aching with the effort of trying to save his life. But no amount of tugging or twisting worked; the canopy just stayed as it was – a billowing bag of material that looked more like an air sock than something that would prevent him being totalled on the ground below.

A *ping* sounded amidst the flapping. It shattered Ethan's panic like glass. His mind cleared and he checked the audible altimeter on his wrist. He'd just zipped past three thousand feet.

At last, Ethan's months of intensive training since finishing his AFF and becoming a proper skydiver kicked in. He saw clearly what he had to do. He had to cut away; get rid of his main canopy.

Skydivers could go their whole life without ever having to do a cut away; modern rigs were phenomenally reliable. But you still did the training; every skydiver had to. If you weren't prepared for the worst, then what chance would you have if the worst actually happened? None.

Ethan remembered what Johnny had told him about his own experience of it, that it had been the scariest thing he'd ever done, because it's a conscious decision to get rid of the one thing you've become so dependent on: your main canopy. All you have left is the reserve. And if he left it much longer, the only thing that would be opening it would be his AAD. And depending on something that opens your reserve at under 1,000 feet isn't leaving much room for error. He'd still have to cut away his main anyway; didn't want it to get tangled up with the reserve.

Ethan had asked the obvious question: 'What happens if the reserve fails too?'

Johnny had told him the odds were so nuts that it just didn't happen. Reserves always deployed. But then he'd added, 'Obviously, there's always a first time.'

7

Thanks, Johnny . . .

Ethan took one last look over his head. The main canopy was screwed. It was a hell of a decision. One there was no return from. One he'd hoped he'd never have to make. But what choice did he have?

None.

He cut away . . .

He was in freefall again. Despite being a mess, his canopy had slowed his descent considerably. With it gone Ethan was accelerating again. It felt like the Earth was pulling him towards it, willing him to slam into it like a meteorite.

Once stable again, he reached round to deploy his reserve, then stopped. He hadn't checked the air above him was clean – what if his main canopy was still directly above, chasing him down to the ground? Deploy now and he'd find himself smacking straight back into it. And if that happened . . .

Ethan checked above, left, right . . .

The main was off to the left and dangerously close. Ethan knew he had to get out of its way. He was also becoming increasingly aware of just how close the ground now was. Even more so when his altimeter pinged again at 2,000 feet.

Ethan swept his arms back and jetted himself out of the way of his main, tracking across the sky like a falcon after its prey. Now he was safe. This was it.

Crack!

The reserve blasted out. It grabbed air and inflated instantly, yanking Ethan from terminal velocity to a slow, controlled descent.

Ethan was utterly speechless. He'd just done his first cut away; it wasn't the kind of moment that came with a pre-recorded list of awesome quotes to impress the chicks. Though he had a feeling Johnny would've come up with something.

Gripping the steering lines, he checked that his heading was OK, adjusting his course to make sure he wasn't about to come in across another skydiver's line and screw up their landing. He was aiming for the fields to the right of the DZ. He'd landed there before when he was training, but this was a little bit different; he'd just saved his own life!

Adrenaline burned through his veins, but Ethan didn't know which emotion was stronger: the sense of relief that he wasn't about to die, or the excitement that he'd nailed a cut away.

The ground came up quicker under his reserve than his main and Ethan felt his heart thumping hard. He pulled on the lines to flare the reserve and slow it down, but it didn't have much effect.

He felt like his whole body was shaking with every beat. He lifted his legs up. For a second or two, the soles of his shoes cut through the long grass with a swishing sound, then they found earth.

Ethan skidded, sunk his backside onto the ground and, as he came to a halt, let out a yell that sent a flock of birds to scatter from the field about him like streamers from a party popper.

Lying back on the ground, he stared up at the sky. A dusting of clouds danced high above like they were trying to impress someone. A shout came from over by the DZ.

'Eth!'

Ethan sat up, flipped round onto his knees, started to

pull his rig in, lines first, then the reserve. Jogging across the field towards him was another skydiver. He was wearing wraparound shades and his shoulder-length blond hair bounced in the air like it was trying to get the world's attention.

This was Johnny, the biggest ego ever to walk the planet, a fantastically talented skydiver – and a great mate.

'Just wanted to check that I didn't need to find another housemate. You OK?'

Despite the joke, Ethan could tell Johnny was concerned. On the outside he didn't seem to have a care in the world, but on the inside he cared deeply, particularly about his friends. And for Ethan, the fact that he was moving into Johnny's flat that very evening helped tear his thoughts away from what he'd just done and focus on normal life. He'd finished packing that morning before heading out. Now all he had to do was get home, load up and move in.

'It was scary as hell,' he said, 'but I'm alive.'

Standing up, he threw his reserve canopy and steering lines over his shoulder. Then he made to head off back to FreeFall, the skydiving centre.

'You left it pretty late,' said Johnny, stepping in beside Ethan. 'What happened? Trying out some freestyle?'

'Panicked and got wrapped up in trying to sort out the lines on my main.'

'Easy to do. Terrifying, isn't it?'

Ethan nodded. 'Not something I'm keen to repeat.'

He then felt Johnny rest his arm across his shoulders and looked up to see a smirk; a sure sign he was about to walk down Johnny-is-God alley.

'Of course, when I did it? Textbook, Eth.'

'A perfect cut away?' said Ethan, not even attempting to hide the sarcasm. 'Amazing.'

'Totally,' said Johnny.

'How is it that none of this brilliance goes to your head?'

'Thankfully, one of my greatest attributes is my modesty.'

Laughing and chatting about the cut away, Ethan and Johnny walked on, taking a wide berth of the DZ to keep out of the way of other skydivers, and headed round to FreeFall itself. It may have looked like nothing more than a collection of knackered hangars and buildings that should've been condemned years ago, but to Ethan it had become a second home since he'd started working there over the previous summer. And now, despite being back at college for his final year, it was all that really mattered. The thrill of skydiving, the friends he'd made, the new direction his life now had. He'd pass his college exams, of that he was sure, but they'd lost their significance. He belonged in the air, and no badly dressed careers advisor or lecturer was going to make him see his life any differently.

Ahead, the rest of the team were waiting for him, sitting outside the café on a bench. It was Luke who approached him first and, as ever, he was immaculately turned out. Ethan half wondered if Luke had a nice clean jumpsuit for every day of the week; his own was already looking a little worn in places, but Luke's was never anything but pristine.

Luke held out his hand and smiled; a strange mix of politeness and warmth.

'That was a bit close, Ethan,' he said as Ethan shook his hand. 'Most people don't get to do a cut away for years, never mind in their first few months. Well done on giving up on your canopy and going for your reserve.'

'Thanks,' said Ethan.

Luke then stood back, arms folded, like he was appraising Ethan.

'Do we know who the rigger was? We should trace it back and find out. A cut away could be a random event, or – and more frighteningly – because someone didn't do their job properly.'

'Do you ever stop?' asked Johnny. 'Do you sleep at night, or do you go around checking the wiring in all your plugs, or making sure any envelopes you might use won't give anyone a paper cut?'

Luke's face didn't crack. 'Devil's in—'

'The detail,' finished Johnny.

'You should be very proud,' said Natalya, pushing back her red hair and handing Ethan something to drink. He still hadn't been able to work out where she was from, her eastern European accent not pinning her down to anywhere specific. 'It is a difficult thing to do, to keep a level head in such a situation. You have done well.'

Ethan never quite knew how to take Natalya's compliments. They were never given with much in the way of emotion, more a statement of fact. Everything about her seemed slightly guarded, like she was hiding something. Even the way she walked looked calculated rather than relaxed, almost as though she was always ready to bolt. And Ethan didn't fancy his or anyone else's chances at keeping up with her; she was built like a gazelle.

He sipped his drink, then looked over to Kat. He may not

have been all that sure yet of Natalya, but Kat was easier to read than a tabloid, and he liked that, well, more than liked it actually, not that he'd let on quite yet. Didn't want to mix work and pleasure.

Kat smiled. As always, it lit up her face like a firework.

'You still feeling the adrenaline?'

'Totally,' said Ethan, sitting down next to her. His leg momentarily touched hers and for a split second he wasn't exactly sure which was more exciting: jumping out of a plane, or the idea of him and Kat. 'My fingers are still tingling.'

A very distinctive sound trampled any further conversation dead.

'Sam's here,' said Luke, stating the obvious as the roar of an engine thundered through the air. 'Let's see what he thinks.'

Ethan glanced over to see Sam's huge black Defender skid to a halt. Then the man himself jumped out and made straight for him, his face as dark as an approaching storm.

2

Ethan stood up and tried to make himself look as tall as possible. It didn't work. Sam didn't just have the height advantage, he was huge all over; it was like standing in front of a bear. The shadow he cast under the afternoon sun blacked out Ethan's world and he shivered.

'What happened?'

Sam's gruff voice always got to the point. He wasn't one for niceties.

'I had to cut away,' said Ethan, stating the obvious. Under Sam's stare, he felt like everything he was about to say was going to sound stupid and wrong.

'Why?'

Ethan felt his throat closing up. How did Sam have this power?

'The exit looked fine,' said Sam. 'Formations were spot-on. When you broke away, that was textbook.'

At last, Ethan found his voice. 'I think it was a line over,' he said, doing his best to use the right terminology, not just to impress Sam and the rest of the team, but also to make himself feel better; he wanted to show he knew what he was talking about and that he'd done well in the circumstances. But on hearing his own voice he wasn't convincing even himself. 'One of the lines passed in front of the canopy, I mean the nose. The air couldn't get in to inflate it properly.'

'Sure?'

'Yes,' said Ethan, working hard to sound confident. Thinking back over what had happened, he knew it was the only explanation. He just wasn't sure he'd explained it clearly enough.

'You handled it well, Ethan,' said Sam, 'once you'd made the cutaway. But you took too long to do it. You know that, right?'

Ethan knew it better than he knew anything. Just the thought that he'd left it really tight made him go cold; he'd been only seconds away from a bounce that would've killed him. It was a chilling thought.

'I got too focused on my rig,' he said, trying not to let that feeling of fear show in his voice. 'I know I shouldn't have done, but it's not the same when you're up there and it actually happens.'

Ethan wanted to kick himself. That last comment had sounded like an excuse. It wasn't. He was just trying to say . . . oh crap, what the hell was he trying to say?

Sam's voice brought him out of his thoughts.

'You lost altitude awareness.'

'Yeah,' said Ethan. 'It was the ping from my altimeter as I burned through three thousand that brought me round. Then the training kicked in.'

'It's supposed to,' growled Sam. 'Just not so bloody late in the day, got it?'

Everything Sam said felt like a punch in the gut. But Ethan knew he had to *man it up*, as Johnny would say. Sam was hard on them because he knew better than any of them the risks involved.

'The rest of you take note,' said Sam, and Ethan watched him swing round to look at the team, saw them all flinch just a little. 'Ethan was lucky up there today. No matter how rare cut aways actually are, he's just demonstrated that one'll bite you on your arse without any warning. Understand?'

Ethan, like the rest, said, 'Yes, Sam.' They felt and sounded like schoolchildren in trouble with their teacher.

'Never lose altitude awareness. Always follow your training. It's that simple and that important.'

No one responded.

Sam looked at them all in turn, then said, 'Right, into the hangar, all of you. Let's run through Johnny's film of the jump and find out what else went wrong. And then once we've done that, I want to tell you about a little break from the norm I've arranged.'

Johnny sighed. 'Great. A two-week holiday in a hole in the ground, shitting into plastic bags, right? I remember the last time you took us on holiday.'

Ethan wasn't sure, but he thought he saw the faint flicker of a smile dare to chance its way across Sam's face. He said,

'But I thought we were training for when the competition season starts up again in the spring?'

Ethan was loving the fact that despite being so new to the sport, he would be doing his first proper competitions with the team in a few months. He wouldn't be doing solo stuff or freestyle, but formation. And he was completely focused on not simply getting everything right, but *perfect*.

'We are,' said Kat. 'But sometimes it's good to take a break. And despite what Luke thinks, it stops you making errors by focusing too much on the detail.'

'But what about the competitions?' asked Ethan, unable to avoid the fact that he felt he was going to be hard-pushed to match the skills of the rest of the team come their first competitive jump. 'Won't a break in practising set us back?'

Sam spoke again, looking directly at Ethan. 'Your skydiving is fine. And like Kat said, it will do you good to have a break.'

Ethan went to say something, but thought better of it.

'So for a few days you're going to skill up in other areas.'

'Like what?'

'You'll find out soon enough,' said Sam. 'And it'll be a serious test to take you to the next level, give you a chance to keep up with the rest of the team on these skills. It's tough but you'll survive.'

Ethan had only just survived a cutaway. He didn't much like the idea of having to take part in something else which involved the same sensation.

Sam looked back round at the rest of the team. 'As for the rest of you, this is revision.'

Ethan felt Kat's shoulders slump a little against his.

She looked suddenly not just serious, but a little worried. In fact, they all did. He turned to Johnny and said under his breath, 'What does he mean by the next level? What's going on?'

What Sam had just said made him a little nervous. When it came to 'tough', he knew Sam meant something a little more extreme than the rest of humanity.

When Johnny spoke next, his voice had lost his usual jokiness. 'It's quite simple; Sam's about to take us somewhere wet, muddy and cold, and do his best to make us feel like he's actually trying to kill us.'

Ethan felt Kat's hand tap his thigh. 'It's a learning experience. At least that's what we're supposed to think.' She glanced up at Sam. 'Couldn't you just take us away for a nice hot beach holiday?'

Ethan laughed, not just at the thought of Sam doing something so completely out of character, but also to disguise the fact that all he could now think of was seeing Kat in a bikini.

'I've arranged a two-week intensive course to cover the basic skills you all need to help you survive hostile situations. Your cover story is simple; like Ethan said, you're all training for the new competition season next year. So as far as anyone else is concerned, you're away doing two weeks of intensive jumping somewhere with better weather than the UK.'

'We're going abroad?' said Ethan. Now that, he liked the sound of. But he saw Johnny shaking his head.

'I doubt that, mate,' he said. 'We get to stay here while our imaginary selves are skydiving in Gap, in France. Doesn't seem very fair, does it?'

Sam said, 'I've enlisted the expertise of a few of my

contacts to make sure that this is as real as it gets. I know I'm preaching to the converted, but be assured that you will be pushed beyond what you ever thought you were capable of, and then pushed some more.' He paused then said, 'Prepare yourselves to be hungry, cold, knackered and at points – assuming I've done my job right – bloody scared.'

Ethan was starting to feel even more nervous and did his best to make sure it didn't show. He knew full well that Sam was more than capable of scaring him half to death. He had a horrible sinking feeling that the cutaway would have nothing on what Sam's imagination could dream up.

Luke coughed. 'When are we going?'

A crinkled smile definitely appeared on Sam's face and Ethan knew better than he knew anything else that it meant trouble.

'Welcome to your first test,' Sam said, looking at each of them in turn. 'We leave tomorrow. So use the cover story and get out of whatever it is you have planned from now until we come back.'

Words jumped from Ethan's mouth before he had a chance to stop his thoughts being said aloud: 'But I'm moving into Johnny's tonight and we're having the house-warming party tomorrow!'

'You can still move in,' said Johnny. 'We'll just have to postpone the knees-up.'

Ethan couldn't help but feel disappointed. Moving out of his family's flat was a big step, and the party was as much a part of it as the actual unloading of boxes. And he'd been looking forward to an evening doing something other than skydiving with the team, particularly with Kat.

Sam wasn't finished. 'Forget asking me any questions,' he said, and Ethan saw him glance at Kat, who was in the process of putting her hand up. 'You will be presented with surprise situations and be expected to react accordingly, both as a team and as individuals. I'm not about to spoil all that by telling you what I've got planned.'

'But—' began Kat.

'But nothing,' Sam replied, and turned for the door. 'Here's your kit list. Get it sorted. And don't take anything that's not on it.'

Then he was gone.

Ethan looked at the list. It was huge.

'Sorry about the party,' said Kat. 'I was really looking forward to it.'

'Sam can be a bit of git at times, can't he?' said Ethan. 'I bet he's been planning this for ages. Why didn't he just tell us a couple of weeks ago rather than now?'

'He likes to keep us on our toes,' said Kat. 'I was going to remind him that we'd been planning the party for a while, but he didn't give me a chance.'

'I wondered why you had your hand up,' said Ethan. 'Thanks, anyway.'

Kat smiled. 'It's a big step, you moving out. Sam probably doesn't understand how big, but the rest of us do. We'll just have the party when we get back; it'll be brilliant, I promise!'

Ethan felt chuffed to hear Kat cared and also understood. But it still wasn't much of a buffer to what Sam had just said.

'So where are we supposed to get all this stuff?' he asked, nodding at the list. 'Sam always seems to expect the impossible.'

Luke rattled the keys, then strode off to the far end of the hangar. Ethan and the rest followed and found themselves in Sam's storeroom.

'Oh, right,' said Ethan. 'Figures.'

3

Ethan pulled his Land Rover into a parking space which, unlike most of the others, wasn't actually filled with broken bottles and cigarette packets, then heaved on the hand brake. Switching off the engine, he used his shoulder as much as the handle to open the door, and clambered out. Walking away from it, he tapped his hand against the wing. The vehicle was ancient, the canvas roof leaked, and every time he went over a puddle, water splashed up through the floor. The heater didn't work, just rattled, and sometimes the windscreen wipers just gave up altogether. But to Ethan, these were just niggles, little things he had to put up with.

From the moment he'd clapped eyes on Sam's own Defender, he'd wanted one. Granted, he'd known from the off he'd never be able to afford one like that, but with a bit of searching around he'd found a local dealer who'd helped out.

He'd bought it for next to nothing. It was basic, which had allowed him to fix a few problems he'd otherwise have had to go to a garage for, and it was pretty much indestructible. Slow it may have been, but it made enough noise to scare the hell out of anyone laughing at him as they drove past him in their boy racers. Above all, it gave him a way to escape, which was worth more than anything. And tonight, even though the house-warming party was now cancelled, he was taking that final step to true freedom; moving out of the family flat and in with Johnny. Fantastic!

Ethan looked up at the block of flats he'd called home for far too long. Just seeing it standing there, like a dead tree against the sky, made it even more clear to him that moving out wasn't just the *right* decision, it was the *only* one he could actually make. Amazingly, it had been Johnny who'd suggested he move in with him, making it even easier; he hadn't had to look for digs or even save up a deposit. Life, Ethan felt, had sorted it out, and he wasn't going to argue.

A few minutes later, having climbed the concrete stair-well, doing his best not to breathe and avoid the stale stench of urine all the way, he walked along to the flat. From this point on, he thought with a smile, it was no longer home. He was out of here and God, did that taste good. But as the thought of what was to come made Ethan smile, the sight of the front door to the flat snapped the smile in half.

The door, which had clearly been kicked in, was hanging by one hinge, the wind catching it and making it flap against the wall.

Ethan stepped through and into the flat – or what was left of it.

'Mum? Jo?'

The flat was horribly silent, like the place had been swept clean of life by a hurricane.

In the hallway, pictures that had been hanging on the wall were all smashed on the floor. One had a huge dirty boot print on it. Ethan clocked his dad's jacket chucked on the carpet. The sight of it, and the sound of glass from the picture frames crunching under his feet, sent a shiver of rage through him and he clenched his fists.

'Dad . . .'

With each step now, Ethan was more careful. He knew who was responsible for the damage. And if he was still here he was going to be ready for him.

Ethan leaned his head into the kitchen, but he didn't go in. No point; he could see the damage well enough from where he was. It looked like the place had suffered an earthquake. The floor was covered in broken plates and jars of food, shelves had been stripped bare and the fridge light was blinking on and off as the door tried to swing itself shut.

Pulling himself away to walk on, he could almost hear his dad charging through the house; he'd heard it all too often. But this . . . he'd never gone so far before. Usually it had been just another drunken tantrum, a smashed mug or two and that was it. Nothing like this.

Ethan realized then his anger at what he'd found was turning to concern; despite calling out again, he'd got no reply from his mum or his sister. Were they OK? Had his dad completely lost the plot and gone at them too?

Nervous now of what he might find, Ethan headed further down the hallway. The lounge door was open. He glanced in, saw the television on its back, giving the ceiling a nice private viewing of some crappy game show. The sofa was on its side, more pictures had been pulled from the wall and smashed on the floor. Even the curtains had been ripped down. Christ, what had his dad been on to do this?

Ethan moved past the bathroom and to the bedrooms. He called out again. Still no reply. He was finding it hard to stay calm now, but seeing what his dad had done made him cautious. If his dad was still here, he wasn't about to let himself be caught out; he was going to be ready for him.

Ethan came to his own room, easing the door slowly open then letting it go so that it swung right round to hit the wall behind; at least his dad wasn't hiding in here, he thought. But the damage he then saw almost made him wish that he were.

He'd spent hours boxing his belongings up all ready to move to Johnny's, but now he felt like he was staring into the back of a dump truck. Every box had been kicked in, slashed and ripped, his bags emptied, clothes scattered.

Ethan bent down to pick up a broken CD case, the anger burning inside him feeling like it had been doused with petrol. 'Why did you do this, Dad?' he muttered to himself, then a sound made his voice catch in his throat. He listened in, tried to filter out all the other sounds coming through the flat from the open front door. There it was again; someone crying.

Ethan tossed the CD case into the room like a crap

Frisbee and was on his feet and into the hallway. Across from his room was Jo's. He flung the door open; it was in as much a state as the rest of the flat, Jo's artwork and posters scattered and ruined like rubbish washed up on a beach. But it was empty. Ethan turned back to the hallway and ran through the remaining door into his parents' bedroom.

The floor was covered in clothes ripped from the wardrobe, the chest of drawers on its face like a drunk.

'Mum . . .'

She was curled up in a ball on the bed.

Ethan walked over and rested a hand on her arm. At his touch, she flinched.

'Mum, it's me, Ethan. He didn't hurt you, did he? You OK?'

Ethan saw a faint nod of the head.

Ethan sat down. His mum stayed curled up.

'What happened? Why did Dad do this? Where's Jo?'

Ethan felt his mum reach out and rest her hand on his. His emotions were a mess. He wasn't just angry at his dad for what he'd done; he was upset for his mum, for having to put up with the arsehole for all these years, and for having him destroy the home she worked so hard to look after. A part of him wanted to head out right away, find him, and just let rip. But another part told him he had to stay, make sure his mum was OK, sort the flat out. Suddenly moving in with Johnny didn't seem so important, not with everything he'd grown up with now lying in tatters in front of him.

'Jo wasn't here,' said his mum, at last pushing herself up, wiping her face of tears. 'And I'm glad. Your dad, he was drunk, but not like usual. He was uncontrollable, Ethan.'

'Where is he?' Ethan couldn't hide the anger in his voice; it laced every word he said.

'It doesn't matter, Ethan,' said his mum. 'He's gone now.'

'I'll kill him.'

'No, you won't,' his mum replied, looking at Ethan through bloodshot eyes. 'You won't do anything of the sort. Do you understand?'

Ethan didn't understand at all, but he nodded a yes anyway.

'I'm sorry about your room. You spent so long packing up. I'll help you sort it.'

Ethan smiled. Typical Mum, he thought.

A shout came from the hallway and Jo appeared at the door.

'What the hell happened? Where is he? Where's Dad?'

'Not here,' said Ethan. 'Where've you been?'

'Working,' replied Jo, and Ethan didn't just hear the edge in her voice; he felt it. 'With you moving out, someone's got to help out round here, haven't they?'

'You know why I'm moving out,' said Ethan.

'Whatever,' said Jo and went over to her mum. 'Did he hurt you?'

'No, he didn't,' Ethan told her, and stood up.

Jo said, 'Where are going? You're not seriously still thinking of moving out tonight, are you?'

'I'm going to phone the police,' Ethan replied.

He saw his mum start at this and she looked up at him, her face lined with worry and fear. 'No, Ethan, don't do that. We can sort this out. Please . . .'

Ethan looked at Jo. She nodded, rested a hand on her mum's shoulder.

'We have to,' said Ethan. 'This is nothing like what he's done before.'

Decision made, Ethan left the room, found the phone in the hallway under one of the smashed pictures, and punched in a call.

Soon after, the police arrived, checked the damage and took all the details Ethan, Jo and their mum could give on his dad, promising to bring him in as soon as possible. They then called in a community-support officer to keep an eye on the flat, just in case he returned that night. When finally left alone, the three of them set about tidying up. Ethan hadn't forgotten that as of tomorrow he was away with Sam and the rest of the team. He just hadn't quite worked out how to tell his mum and Jo. He really wanted to stay and help them get sorted but, despite what had happened, he knew that missing Sam's training was not an option.

He was in the kitchen with his mum and Jo, and filling the teapot, when his mum said, 'You need to give Johnny a ring.'

'I know,' said Ethan. 'No way am I going to move in tonight, but—'

His mum cut him off. 'No, Ethan, I meant just to tell him why you're late. You need to go. We'll be fine. You've made your decision. Don't let your dad mess it up. Don't give him that power.'

Ethan made to protest.

'I won't hear of it,' said his mum.

'But you'll need the locks changing,' said Ethan. 'Maybe you should come with me, to Johnny's? I'm sure he'd be fine about it. Anyway, we're going to be away for a couple of weeks, so it's not like the place would be crowded.'

'You're what?' said Jo.

Ethan felt like a stone had just dropped into his stomach as he went on with the cover story. 'Sam's taking us away for some intensive skydiving training,' he said. 'We're heading to Gap in France. The weather's better there so we can get more air time.'

'And you only thought to tell us now?'

'I've cleared it with college,' he lied. 'I'm taking my course-work with me.'

'Still doesn't explain why you didn't tell us,' said Jo.

'Because,' said Ethan, 'when Sam told us, I knew I'd have moved in with Johnny, so the fact I was going to be away wasn't really going to be a problem, was it?'

'And you'd have told us how? By postcard?'

Ethan saw his mum shake her head. 'Please,' she said, 'don't argue, you two.'

Jo huffed into her mug of tea and Ethan tried to ignore the dagger eyes she was stabbing him with.

'Ethan, we will be fine. Won't we, Jo?'

'Yes,' said Jo. 'More than.'

'We can sort the flat tomorrow; it's just a bit of tidying up, really, nothing more. And I can get someone to do the locks as well.'

'But Johnny's place is going to be empty,' said Ethan.

'No,' said his mum, and Ethan could tell the argument was over. 'All this is just cosmetic. If anything, I'm pleased it happened; he's forced our hand, hasn't he?'

Ethan said nothing, just listened. He couldn't remember

the last time he'd heard his mum sound so determined.

'He's out of our lives for good now, Ethan. And we're not going to let him ruin this new life of yours, either. Understand?'

Ethan nodded.

'Good,' said his mum. 'Now let's get you packed and off, shall we? The sooner you're out of here, the sooner I can get on with throwing out your dad's stuff, and that's something I've been wanting to do for a very long time indeed.'

4

'Tell me again why you bought this?' asked Johnny, his feet braced against the metal dash of Ethan's Land Rover.

It was early morning, and Ethan and Johnny were only a couple of minutes away from FreeFall and whatever it was that Sam had sorted for the next two weeks. Johnny had attempted to read a skydiving magazine, but given up thanks to the ride from the vehicle being anything but smooth.

Ethan hadn't slept well. After what had happened the night before, and despite every reassurance his mum, and even Jo, had given him that they would be fine, he was still worried. He'd phoned them that morning and they'd already sorted someone to come out to change the locks. And the police had been in touch as well; they hadn't yet found his dad, but were following up some leads and didn't think it would be too long before he was in custody. So, all in all, things sounded sorted. But he still felt bad about heading off for two weeks, not being around if they needed him. But then, perhaps doing this was a better use of his time anyway? He was doing something positive with his life, unlike his point-less loser dad, and through it all he was going to make damned sure he didn't just make life better for himself, but for his mum and Jo too.

'Earth to Ethan,' said Johnny, punching Ethan in the arm.

'Sorry,' said Ethan. 'Just thinking about Mum and Jo.'

'They'll be fine,' said Johnny. 'Your mum's got it all in hand, right? And your dad's got more to think about than just screwing things up for you lot now the police are after him.'

'I know,' said Ethan. 'Still feels like I'm running out on them.'

Ahead of them, FreeFall came into view. Once they'd checked in at the gate with the security guard, they were on the final stretch of road leading up and round to the car park.

'Luke's already here,' said Johnny as Ethan swung his old Land Rover into the car park, the huge tyres spitting grit across the ground. 'Probably been here all night ironing the parachutes and repacking the kit.'

Laughing, Ethan switched off the engine and slid out into the day. Everyone ribbed Luke for his attention to detail, but only because they respected it and depended on it.

The sky was overcast, cloud cover low; a full-on no-jump day. The wind was getting up too, and walking round to the back of his Land Rover, Ethan shivered, pulling his jacket in tight and zipping it up.

'Doesn't exactly bode well, does it?' said Johnny, joining Ethan as he dropped the tailgate. 'If the weather's like this now it's only going to feel worse when Sam's got us wading through bogs up to our necks.'

'You're really not selling it to me,' said Ethan, grabbing his bergen. 'It's not going to be totally horrific, is it?'

Johnny pulled out his own bergen and slammed the tailgate shut. 'Sam's no holiday tour operator,' he said. 'His idea of a good time is to run us ragged, feed us on boil-in-the-bags, and teach us the finer arts of blowing stuff up, CQC and surviving interrogation. Surely he mentioned all this at the job interview?'

'Won't we be skydiving?' asked Ethan, ignoring Johnny's question. 'I know the cover story is that we're skydiving, but he's not going to just let us go jump-dry, is he? We must be doing some, at the very least.'

Johnny waved to Luke who sent a wave back. 'Oh, we'll be in the air,' said Johnny. 'Probably more so than we have been for the past few weeks.'

'So what's not to look forward to, then? Why all the doom and gloom?'

'Because,' said Johnny, 'if I know Sam, then we won't just be doing the usual stuff, right? We'll probably be doing night jumps while he fires RPGs at us.'

Ethan laughed, but also wondered if there was just a little bit of truth in what Johnny had said.

'Night jumps, though,' he said. 'What's not to love? I mean, that's a serious rush and we both know it.'

Just the thought of it made Ethan's fingers tingle. The sensation of leaping out of a plane was almost indescribable, but doing it at night? Well, that was like jumping into nothing, darkness everywhere, the ground below barely visible, a blanket of black dotted by the fairy lights of civilization.

Johnny grinned wide. 'Remember doing it with flares? Now that's awesome.'

'Not much else it can be really, is there?' said Ethan. 'Streaming through the air at night, with your feet on fire, and a hundred-metre stream of white-hot flame burning the sky behind you; can't understand why more people don't do it.'

Johnny rested his hand on Ethan's shoulder. 'Be thankful they don't, mate; can you imagine what it would be like if there were more people in the world like us?'

Ethan laughed. The thought of it was terrifying.

As they walked over to meet Luke, a waft of something delicious drifted by from the FreeFall café.

'Smells like Nancy's in early,' said Ethan. 'We got time to grab something to eat?'

Nancy ran the café and her food was legendary; her bacon butties had become a staple of Ethan's skydiving diet.

'I'm afraid not,' said Luke, meeting them halfway. 'Sam's going to be here in a couple of minutes.'

Ethan had noticed early on how Luke never strolled. Whatever he was doing, he always did it with a sense of purpose.

'Kat and Natalya are on their way as well,' Luke continued. 'And before you ask, yes, I have double-checked all the kit. It's out in the storeroom waiting for us to go in there and grab it.'

'Need me to check your stuff, just in case?' asked Johnny,

dropping his bergen to the ground. 'You know, fresh pair of eyes and all that?'

'No, I think I'm fine, Johnny,' said Luke. 'But thanks for the offer.'

Johnny glanced over at Luke's own bergen. 'Shirts? Waterproofs? Sleeping bag? Spare pants? Steam iron?'

Luke shook his head with a smile. 'So how are you, Ethan?'

'Nervous,' said Ethan, which was true enough, though he wasn't sure if it was simply because he didn't know what Sam had planned, or because he was thinking about his mum and Jo. It was hard not to. 'Johnny's kind of given me the impression it's going to be hell. Loads of running around and getting shot at.'

'And since when do any of us listen to Johnny?' asked Luke.

'That's just because you all fear my wisdom,' said Johnny, folding his arms and nodding his head knowingly.

'Is it?' said Ethan. 'I just thought it was because you talked bollocks.'

Johnny's laugh was drowned out by the arrival of three more vehicles into the car park. The first was Sam's Defender, which made Ethan's own Land Rover look like a very distant, and very knackered, cousin. He was followed by Kat and Natalya. The last was a minibus driven by someone Ethan didn't recognize. The vehicle itself was more rust than anything else. It was hard to see how it was in any way road-legal.

Ethan waved at Kat and was more than a little pleased to get a wave back. Then he looked over at the minibus.

'Who's that?'

'I'm guessing,' said Luke, 'that it's one of Sam's contacts. Which means he's probably ex-special forces, half insane and on a break between high-paid contract jobs out in Iraq.'

While Sam sorted his stuff out, pulling various bags from the back of his vehicle, Kat and Natalya joined Ethan, Johnny and Luke.

'How you doing?' asked Kat, looking at Ethan.

'Fine,' said Ethan. 'Took a while to get all my stuff over to Johnny's, and I'm not really unpacked, but it feels great to have moved out.'

'No,' said Kat. 'I meant about what happened last night at home with your dad.'

Ethan was confused. 'How do you know about that?' he asked.

'Johnny told me,' said Kat. 'I called last night to check you'd moved in OK, but you weren't there and Johnny told me why. He sounded concerned. How are your mum and Jo?'

Ethan said, 'OK, I think. Dad did a real job on the flat.'

Knowing Johnny, and particularly Kat, were actually in any way bothered about what had happened to him, and to Jo and his mum, made Ethan relax a little. He was among friends who were interested in what was going on in his life and he really appreciated that.

'And you? Are you OK?'

'To be honest,' said Ethan, 'I don't know. I was going to stay, but Mum pretty much pushed me out the door.'

Kat laughed, and Ethan knew he could listen to that sound every day. He went to say something else, but Sam turned up then and stood in front of them all, arms folded, his thick forearms looking like knotted ropes.

'Right,' he said. 'Glad you could all make it. Everyone ready?'

Ethan, like the rest of the team, nodded.

'Good,' said Sam. He nodded at the hangar, while heading off towards the cafe. 'No point hanging about, is there? Grab the kit, load up the minibus and we'll get going shortly,' he said over his shoulder.

'Out!'

Ethan blinked, stretched, saw the silhouette of Sam in the open door of the minibus. They'd been on the road for what felt like days and his muscles had seized up. With a yawn, he looked through a grimy window and all he could see was emptiness. Moorland stretched out around the minibus, sweeping up to mountains that broke the clouds high above. The sound of sheep complaining about the weather drifted by on the wind.

'I said, move it!' barked Sam.

Ethan scrambled out after Johnny. The cold air hit him hard and shocked the sleep from his body. He shivered; it was freezing compared with the cozy warmth of the minibus.

'You'll need walking kit,' said Sam, opening the rear of the minibus. 'Boots, fleece, waterproofs. Sort yourselves out and meet me round the back of my Defender.'

Sam strode off and Ethan reached in for his bergen, pulling Johnny's with it. Kat was already pulling her stuff out with Natalya. Luke, it seemed, had second-guessed Sam and was already kitted up and must have got changed on the way in the back of the minibus.

'You know something we don't?' asked Ethan, pulling on his boots, and felt an elbow nudge his arm. It was Kat and she was holding her hand out. 'Energy bars,' she said, her voice hushed, almost a whisper. 'I always carry a few in my jacket, just in case.'

Ethan took them. 'Thanks,' he said, enjoying the conspiracy with Kat. 'We not supposed to have these, then?'

'I just don't want Johnny trying to nick them,' said Kat. 'They don't taste bad and it's always nice to know you've got a little something in case of emergency, right?'

'Yeah,' said Ethan and stowed the bars in his pocket.

'Come on,' said Johnny once the team were ready. 'Sam already sounds like a bear with a sore head.'

A gust of wind blasted Ethan as the team left the shelter of the minibus and jogged over to Sam's Defender. He was holding a box. 'Water and butties,' he said. 'Nancy specials; she got in early this morning to make them. Enough calories to keep you from passing out.'

As each of the team stuffed the provisions into their pockets, Sam pulled out a map. It was in such a sorry state Ethan wondered if it had last been used to wrap up some fish and chips.

Sam jabbed a finger at a red dot on the map. 'You're here. You need to get to here.' He moved his finger to a red 'x' at another point on the map. 'Two hours. Get shifting.'

He said no more. Just handed the map to Natalya, slammed the back door of the Defender, walked round, clambered into the driver's seat and drove off. Not even a blast of the horn. The minibus pulled away after him and the team were alone.

* * *

'I mean this in the best possible way,' said Johnny, 'but what a bastard.'

'What about a compass?' asked Ethan.

'Sam hasn't given us one,' said Luke. 'It's a test – see if we can navigate using just what we can see around us, and this map.' He checked his watch and said, 'I'll keep an eye on the time; don't want to be late and put Sam in a bad mood straightaway, do we?'

Ethan watched as Natalya checked out their surroundings, then reorientated the map. 'This' – she said, her finger on the map, and nodding at a large mountain – 'is that mountain over there. The route to our destination is straight down the valley. I would guess fifteen kilometres.'

The mountain looked huge, thought Ethan, happy that they weren't heading over it, particularly as a wall of rain was sweeping down it and heading directly for them.

'Fifteen?' he said. 'Seriously? In two hours?'

'Do not worry,' said Natalya. 'Running will be fun!'

'How?'

Ethan knew he was fitter than he'd been a few months ago, but a fifteen-kilometre run, particularly as his body was still stiff from the journey, sounded long and painful.

'We have plenty of time,' said Natalya, folding the map away. 'And running here is a lot more interesting than back at home, yes? The scenery is beautiful!'

Ethan wasn't so sure. He liked being fit, but he still had to force himself to go running every week. He just didn't enjoy it. Perhaps Natalya had a point, he thought, looking around him; it certainly was more beautiful than back home, and he wouldn't have to spend most of his time dodging pedestrians and rubbish.

Luke interrupted his thoughts. 'I'll set the pace,' he said, zipping up his jacket. 'We'll change every fifteen minutes to keep ourselves alert. Let's move!'

Johnny folded and stowed the map, and Luke turned and set off at an easy jog. Ethan stepped in at the back of the group. Five minutes later, the rain caught them. And it didn't stop. Not even when Johnny, who'd nominated himself as Morale Officer and sung various apparently motivational songs from *Full Metal Jacket*, moved on to 'Singin' in the Rain'.

When the singing ended, Luke called back to Ethan with, 'Eth, your turn to take over.'

Ethan upped his pace to bring himself to the front, and Luke dropped back. Now, with just the road ahead, rather than the backs of the heads of the rest of the team, he thought about what Natalya had said; this really was a whole lot more fun than the usual route he took when he was doing his regular runs back home. The air was fresh, the mountains and moors beautiful. And leading the team forward, he made a note to himself that once a week at least he'd drive out of town and run in the countryside.

The miles melted away. The rain drenched them, but by taking it in turns to set the pace, it broke down the run into easy chunks that raced by.

When they finally arrived at their destination, Ethan didn't feel half as knackered as he'd expected. He wolfed the food and water Nancy had prepared, but kept the energy bars Kat had given him. He might need those for another time.

Sam was waiting for them, standing in the entrance of a large, green canvas tent.

The team jogged over. On the way, Ethan looked around the site. It was a grassy clearing surrounded by woodland on three sides. Besides Sam's Defender and the minibus, another truck had joined them. It looked military and tough as hell. Around the clearing were various tents and crates covered in tarpaulins. It looked like a set piece for an eighties action movie.

'You're on time,' Sam growled. 'Maybe I was too easy on you.'

Ethan was sweating like a pig on a spit. If this was Sam going easy on them, he had a sneaking suspicion the time ahead was going to be much harder. And a whole lot more exhausting.

'This is the briefing tent. You'll eat in here as well, but we'll also use it to explain tasks, debrief, etcetera. You've all got individual tents just behind here. Your stuff has already been put in them. For cleaning up, you'll find two other tents – one for the lads, one for Kat and Natalya – over by the portaloos. You've got half an hour to sort yourselves out before I want you back here. Any questions?'

5

The rain had turned to drizzle. Ethan followed the team round to the tents and quickly found which one was his. It, like the others, was a green A-frame tent with aluminium poles. The inner tent was lined with horizontal straps to hang gear from. It was large enough, Ethan thought, to take at least four others.

'Nice pad,' said Johnny, ducking his head in. 'The inner tent has a heat-retaining coating on it. They're actually arctic tents, usually used by the Paras and the Marines, but perfect for the kind of weather we get here.'

Ethan smiled. 'You sound like Luke.'

'Seriously, shoot me,' said Johnny. 'You did well with the run, Eth. Nice one.'

'Thanks. It was your singing that kept me going. What do you reckon we'll be doing next?'

Johnny shrugged. 'The jog was nothing more than a warm-up. A nice simple team-building exercise to get us all focused on why we're here.'

'I love the fact we're seeing a fifteen-kilometre run as a warm-up,' said Ethan. 'I wouldn't have said that six months ago.'

'Six months ago, you weren't even skydiving,' said Johnny. 'And I bet that seems even more incredible.'

Ethan unclipped the lid of his bergen, and in some vain attempt to make himself feel more at home started to unpack. 'I sometimes wonder just what the hell I was doing with my life,' he said, pulling his things out and resting them on the canvas groundsheet of the tent. 'It's not like I've got much to show for it.'

'If you're going to get all philosophical,' said Johnny, slipping back out through the tent door, 'I'll leave you to it. Just make sure you stay alert, OK? Sam has a nasty habit of springing stuff on us to keep it interesting.'

Then he was gone and Ethan was alone.

Stripping out of his sweat-soaked clothes, Ethan hung them from some of the straps closest to the door to dry. He had a feeling that washing them wasn't going to be an option until either they were back home or the clothes simply disintegrated.

Warm and dressed in dry gear again, and with his tent in some semblance of order, Ethan headed back to the briefing tent. Pushing through the door flap, he wondered exactly what Sam was going to throw at them next. Whatever it was, he had to admit he was pretty excited about it. But then that came with the territory; hanging out with the rest of the team was never something he could call dull, not when most times he was only a few feet away from them and plummeting to the earth at 120 mph.

'Ethan! Catch!'

Ethan looked round just in time to stop an onion cracking him in the skull, catching it in his left hand.

'It's self-catering,' said Johnny from the other end of the briefing tent. He was waving a large ladle. 'It's like our very own version of *Ready, Steady, Cook*!'

Half an hour later the team were sitting down and eating. Ethan did his best not to just sling the food down his neck, even though he was starving. He didn't want to risk giving himself stomach cramps if Sam had them out running again.

'Here,' said Kat, passing something to Ethan. 'It'll help whatever it is we're eating taste of something.' Ethan looked down to see a large bottle of Tabasco sauce in his hands. 'Remember,' said Kat, 'that Johnny cooked this. It needs all the help it can get.'

Ethan splashed the sauce over his remaining food and soon his mouth was almost on fire.

Kat flashed her killer smile. 'Any better?'

'Hot stuff,' said Ethan, reaching for his water.

'Thanks,' said Kat, 'but I was talking about the sauce!'

Ethan laughed, but it was cut short as Sam marched into the tent. The space suddenly felt much smaller, particularly when, almost on Sam's heels, two other men entered.

The first, Ethan and the rest of the team recognized. He was the driver who'd brought them here. He was small, slim and in the strange light of the tent, with evening drawing on outside, looked like a collection of broken sticks and branches covered in combat gear, almost as though a farmer had dressed up a scarecrow in army surplus. But his eyes had a meanness to them, thought Ethan, and the muscles of his forearms were ropes of wire and looked strong enough to rip your arms off with just a twist.

The other man was a giant, taller even than Sam. He looked like a rugby player, with a smashed nose and damaged ears. Ethan wondered how on earth someone like him bought clothes.

'Now,' said Sam, nodding at the two men, 'allow me to introduce you to your instructors for your time out here.'

The two men stayed exactly where they were, still as statues.

'You've all met Reg,' said Sam, nodding at the driver. 'And this is Mal.'

Neither man spoke.

'Don't look exactly friendly, do they?' whispered Johnny, leaning in to Ethan.

'They're not here to be friendly, Johnny,' said Sam, almost cutting Johnny off.

Ethan made a mental note to never whisper anything at a meeting led by Sam. He had the ears of a bat. And a stare that could burn your face off.

'Reg joined the Paras at seventeen. Went for Selection three years later. He's served all over the world, and is an expert in pretty much everything you could imagine that involves either staying alive, or making sure other people don't.'

45

Ethan looked at Reg. He wasn't sure, but had the man actually blinked even once since entering the tent?

'Mal,' said Sam, 'was in the Royal Marines, went through Selection and served with the Special Boat Service.

'Their instructions are simple. Train you well and push you hard. The situations you'll be put in will test how you react to high stress and pressure. This is not the usual role-play bollocks you'd get if you worked in an office. This will be as close to real as we can make it without actually killing you.' Sam paused. 'Though at times you might think that's exactly what we're trying to do.'

'Thanks for the motivational speech,' said Johnny.

'I'm not here to motivate you,' Sam replied. 'That is up to you. I'm here to make sure, with the help of Mal and Reg, that if you get sent into a life-threatening situation, either by throwing you out of a plane, or by any other means we think appropriate, you get to come out alive.'

Johnny opened his mouth to speak, but Natalya leaned across the table towards him and said simply, 'I think that from now on you should be quiet, Johnny.'

Standing up, Sam stared down at the team. 'You are all here because I chose you. Remember that. You wouldn't be here if I didn't think you had what it takes. I'm not expecting you to get everything right, but I am expecting you to bloody well try.'

Mal stepped forward. 'Like Sam explained,' he said, 'we're here to push you, to test your abilities to adapt and survive and work as a team as well as individuals.'

Ethan noticed how Mal's voice was surprisingly quiet for such a giant of a man. And as he continued to speak, Ethan thought how there was an unshakeable quality to it. He imagined Mal would always speak like that, even with a gun at his head.

'You'll have to use your initiative and work under pressure,' continued Mal, folding his enormous arms across his chest like he was trying to tie a boa constrictor snake in knots. 'From what Sam's told us, and what we've seen ourselves, we know you can all skydive as well as anyone I've ever seen in the air.'

That comment made Ethan feel good. Praise from men like these, he knew for sure, was hard-won.

'You're a great team, used to working together, and that's why your cover story is so damned watertight. But we now want to work on what you're like as individuals. And that's a different ball game altogether.'

Mal stepped back and Reg moved forward to take centre stage. He gave them a smile, but Ethan couldn't help but think that it wasn't one entirely filled with warmth.

'We're going to spend a bit of time looking at how you cope when you've got no one else to rely on but yourself,' he said, his voice less restrained than Mal's. 'It's a different set of skills and you need them just as much as you need the ones you use as a team.'

Reg went quiet and it was back to Sam.

'That's it for now,' he said and made to leave the tent, turning just before he stepped outside. 'One final bit of advice; get your heads down now. It's early evening; make the most of it.'

'Which means,' said Johnny as Sam, Reg and Mal left the tent, 'we probably won't sleep again until the journey home.'

Just a few minutes later Ethan, like the rest of the team, had taken Sam's advice, and he was back in the warmth of his tent, burrowed deep and cosy into his duck-down sleeping bag. The self-inflating camping mat he was lying on was surprisingly comfortable. The wet kit he'd hung up earlier had already started to dry and he figured would be pretty much fine by the morning.

Judging by what Sam, Mal and Reg had said, the next few days were going to be tough. Ethan was nervous, but he was also looking forward to just getting stuck in. He'd learned so much about himself, what he was capable of, since he'd first met Sam and the team, and being away now felt natural. This was what he wanted to do with his life, wasn't it? He wasn't about to start complaining.

Ethan closed his eyes and drifted off to sleep; it was easy in the peace and quiet of the place, with nothing but the sound of the wind slipping through the trees outside.

At no point was he expecting to be pulled from his sleep just a few hours later, by a screaming Reg, with the sound of thunder and rain outside like the world was about to end.

6

'Out! Out! Out!'

Ethan shook the sleep from his head. It was still dark and that disorientated him a little. After what Sam had said about getting some sleep, he'd half expected to wake up in daylight. Instead, he'd been shouted awake just a few hours after dropping off.

Ethan knew it was just an exercise, but that didn't mean he could take it easy, so he grabbed his almost-dry kit from the gear straps, rammed his boots on, pulled up his hood and dashed out into the night. It was soot-black outside and the rain was hammering hard. It felt like someone was throwing ball bearings at him and he pulled his hood even tighter round his face.

Halfway to the briefing tent, Ethan felt a gust of wind catch at him. But there was a sound to it as well, a thrumming in the blackness. He recognized it at once: helicopter blades.

Without breaking his stride, Ethan turned to see a helicopter coming in to land just away from the campsite, sheathed in moonlight and rods of rain. The sight of it in the darkness, shattered only by blasts of lightning, made Ethan's heart quicken. The only reason it was here at all was because it had something to do with whatever he was about to do next. Did that mean they were jumping? But a night jump in this weather? Was that at all possible?

Ethan barged into the briefing tent, quickly followed by Natalya. Luke and Johnny were already inside, as was Sam. Someone was missing though.

'Where's Kat?' asked Ethan, sitting down next to Johnny. But it was Sam who answered.

'I've already briefed her,' he said. 'So don't go thinking she's grabbing a bit of extra shuteye because I'm going soft. Listen up, and we'll get on with what the rest of you are doing.'

Ethan noticed how, even though they all knew this was an exercise, the team were treating it just as seriously as anything else they'd done. But then that was how Sam had trained them, wasn't it? To treat everything as though you're doing it for real, even if it's just rehearsing skydiving formations on the ground. That way, your mind is automatically ready and alert.

Sam brought out a map and a selection of black-and-white photographs. 'This is a hostage rescue. Nice and simple – well, it would be if it wasn't for the crap throwing itself out of the sky.'

The photos were of an old farmhouse sat huddled up next to a small lake like it was trying to hide behind it. It looked like no one had lived in it for years. The map showed the location of the farm, the patch of blue of the lake clearly visible in the centre, with some black squares next to it: the farmhouse and the farm buildings surrounding it.

'Luke, Nat,' said Sam, drawing everyone's attention to the photographs and the map, 'you're on reconnaissance. You will be on the Pinzgauer and dropped two clicks south of the target destination, the farmhouse.'

'Pinzgauer?' asked Ethan.

'It's the mean-looking truck outside,' said Johnny. 'The one that makes even Sam's Defender look a little bit afraid.'

Sam rested his finger near the blue of the lake on the map. Ethan could tell by the look on Luke's face that every single thing Sam said was not only going in, but being analysed and understood.

Johnny looked just as focused. He may have been the joker in the group, but Ethan had always been impressed that he could just switch that part of himself off and get on with the job in hand.

Natalya was calm. He couldn't remember ever seeing her flustered. She seemed to walk through life as though she knew something the rest of the world didn't, and whatever it was gave her an edge. Then his mind turned to Kat. Sam hadn't said anything about what she was doing, other than that he'd briefed her. What was it that Sam had got her doing?

'Your job,' continued Sam, breaking Ethan's trail of thought, 'is to secure the place for Ethan and Johnny. You'll all stay in touch with each other through a chat-net. And you'll all be wearing tactical throat mics. Nat and Luke will be eyes on and will make sure you know exactly what you're facing: number of x-rays, location, hazards, possibles on where the hostage is.

'You'll be flown out on the bird outside. You'll do a night jump at ten thousand feet to a designated DZ – the far side of the lake, hide your rigs, tab in and rescue the hostage. Contact with any x-rays is to be avoided. You'll then RV with Nat and Luke to be picked up at this point here. Questions?'

No one said a word.

'Good,' said Sam. 'And if you were wondering about Kat; she's the hostage.'

'Remember to do under your cuffs, back of your neck and between your fingers,' said Johnny as Ethan, now dressed in his black suit for the night jump, with black grippers at the elbows and knees for another skydiver to grip onto if they were in formation, blacked himself up in what they all called 'war paint', the camouflage cream they used for working at night. 'They're easily missed and stand out if you get pinged by a torch.'

Sam had done a quick recap of the ins and outs of a night jump. Ethan knew it all, had done a number of night jumps anyway, but a quick bit of revision from the master himself was good. And it made him all the more confident in what he was about to do. Then Sam'd left them alone to get kitted up.

All the equipment they needed for the night jump was laid out on one of the tables in the briefing tent, but there was no point putting any of it on until they were absolutely sure no skin would be visible during the op.

Just then, as Ethan did a final check for any bits he'd missed, a head appeared round the tent-flap door. It was Reg.

'Three minutes,' was all he said, then he was gone.

Ethan looked at Luke and Nat. They were also in black kit and looked ready for anything. They were each wearing a small backpack with webbing.

'What kit are you taking with you?' he asked.

'Essential survival equipment,' said Luke, adjusting the straps. 'Medical items, emergency rations.'

'You expecting the worst?'

Luke shook his head. 'It's good practice to always be ready for every eventuality,' he said. 'Doesn't matter if we probably won't need any of it. If we train with it, get used to always having it around, then we'll find it easier to use if we have to in a live situation.'

Natalya checked her chat-net was working, squeezing together the dual transponders – the mics – against her throat and saying her name a couple of times.

'You're coming across nice and clear,' said Johnny. 'Try yours, Eth.'

Ethan copied, then Luke and Johnny did the same.

Satisfied, Luke and Natalya turned to leave the tent, then Natalya turned back to face Ethan and Johnny. 'We will see you at the farmhouse. Do not try anything clever, yes?'

Then Luke added, 'Just get Kat out, nice and clean.'

Johnny nodded. 'I don't do it any other way.'

Then Luke and Nat were gone.

Johnny handed Ethan a skydiving rig and helped him strap it on, checking everything was clipped in right.

'How you feeling?'

'Fine. Better than fine actually, now that we're jumping.'

Johnny reached for the rest of the kit on the table and handed Ethan goggles, an audible altimeter that let out a *ping* for every 1,000 feet fallen, an LED, a rubberized torch and a hook knife to cut away the canopy if it got in a real state before then deploying the reserve. The LED, which Ethan quickly strapped to his leg, was a light visible for up to three miles that anyone doing a night jump had to wear by law. He knew it would stop him getting slammed in the sky by aircraft or any other skydiver jumping with him: in this case, Johnny. The torch, hung by some cord to Ethan's rig and tucked into a pocket to stop it flapping, was for him to use to do a quick check of the canopy and make sure it had deployed correctly.

Ethan said, 'I know I've done night jumps before – we all have – but I've never jumped out of a helicopter. What's it like?'

'It's the airspeed mainly,' Johnny explained. 'With a helicopter in hover, you're jumping from a stationary object, so it's more like BASE jumping when you exit. It also means you can be more accurate when you do a jump as you can hover over the DZ instead of flying right over it. Good for restricted DZs such as oil platforms and the tops of buildings where you haven't got room for error in where you land. Because, as you know, we're always trying to land on them, aren't we?'

'Who jumps first?'

'We jump together,' said Johnny. 'That way we avoid the risk of colliding, and we can break off to safe air nice and easily to deploy.'

The tent door flapped open. It was Sam.

'Shift it,' he said. 'Liftoff is now!'

Ethan was immediately outside and running behind Johnny, slipping his goggles over his eyes, heading for the helicopter. The rain, thankfully, had eased a little, the clouds breaking and now and again letting the moon poke through; at least they wouldn't get completely drenched.

Johnny jumped in, pulled Ethan behind him. Only when the helicopter lifted did Ethan realize that the pilot was Sam. The man, it seemed, could do anything.

As they cut through the air, heading to where they'd jump, Ethan soaked up the experience. In a plane, you were shut off from the outside world till the door opened and you were out. But in a helicopter it was totally different. With the side fully exposed, the wind raced through and Ethan felt so much closer to what they were doing. And he understood totally why the machines were nicknamed birds: it felt like they were riding on the back of one.

Johnny buzzed him on the chat-net. 'You OK?'

Ethan nodded, squeezed the dual transponders, said, 'Yeah. Totally.'

Johnny then tried to raise a response from Luke and Natalya. 'No answer,' he said. 'We must be out of range.'

'That a problem?'

'No,' said Johnny. 'We'll be fine once we land and make for the farmhouse.'

Ethan suddenly felt the helicopter lose forward

momentum and go to hover. Sam gave the call through on the chat-net that it was time to jump.

'Johnny, Ethan; this is the DZ. However, the situation is now critical: Luke and Natalya have been captured en route to the farmhouse. The job is still on. Adapt.'

Ethan wasn't given time to think about the implications of what he'd just heard as Johnny grabbed him and took him to the open door.

'Change frequency,' he said, and they both quickly changed the band they had been using on the chat-net.

They rested their legs over the edge of the opening and activated their LEDs. Ethan felt Johnny grab his arm. He grabbed Johnny's.

And then they were out into the night.

Ethan felt his stomach go. Johnny's description was totally accurate; the sensation was just like doing a BASE jump. But for a BASE jump he'd leaped from a few hundred feet, whereas now he'd just jumped from 10,000. He would definitely be at terminal velocity when he deployed.

Rain was still in the air and it stung his skin. He was holding both of Johnny's arms and it felt as though they weren't falling at all, just hovering in a vast dark space as the wind tried to pull them apart.

Ethan heard both his and Johnny's altimeters ping. It was time to break free. He let go of the grippers on Johnny's sleeves and Johnny did the same.

Ethan tracked right, Johnny left. With a quick check to make sure he was out of Johnny's way, Ethan signalled with a wave off to Johnny that he was about to deploy, then went for his ripcord. For a second, he remembered the cut away last time, how close he'd been to bouncing, but he forced the memory away and went for it.

The loud *crack!* of the canopy, opening above and inflating as it grabbed air and pulled him from 120 mph to 10 mph in less than ten seconds, filled Ethan with relief. He gripped his torch and swept the beam of light over his head to check the darkness above; the canopy was fine, no lines tangled. Now all he had to do was land safely. And at the DZ.

The lake Ethan had seen on the map and on the photographs was dead easy to spot; with the rain now little more than spitting, some moonlight was breaking through the drifting clouds and reflecting on the surface of the water. He adjusted his heading to get himself on course.

Johnny's voice buzzed the air as he spoke over the chat-net. 'Everything OK?'

Ethan squeezed the throat mic. 'Yeah,' he said. 'That was a bit of a rush, though. Night jumps are just so bloody scary!'

'You're not going to cry on me now, are you?'

Ethan laughed. 'Spotted the farmhouse yet?'

'I'm not blind,' said Johnny. They could see light spilling from the windows of a building below them; it had to be the farmhouse.

'That's reassuring.' Ethan adjusted his canopy again. The DZ was only a few seconds away now.

'You go in first,' said Johnny. 'You're in front of me, anyway.'

A few moments later Ethan pulled his feet up and touched down gently to the ground. He quickly killed the canopy, to stop it dragging him along with it and into the lake, balling it up into his arms. As he did so, he saw Johnny come in just a few metres away from him. He ran over.

'Nice landing, Eth.'

'Yeah. Where do you reckon we should hide our rigs?'

Johnny threw Ethan a small package. He unzipped it and unfolded a silk sack large enough to take both rigs. Ethan unclipped himself and bunged his rig in the sack. Johnny did the same.

'Those bushes over there will do,' nodded Johnny.

Ethan hid the rigs then looked across the lake to the farmhouse. 'Pretty lonely place,' he said.

'I'm guessing the nightlife sucks,' said Johnny. 'Come on.' He immediately broke into a run, heading off to circle the lake and come round to the farmhouse.

Adrenaline pushing him on, Ethan chased through the dark after Johnny. With what had happened to Natalya and Luke, he knew that the mission had changed drastically. It made him a little nervous, but he knew that was a good thing; exercise or not, being overconfident wasn't just stupid: it was dangerous.

7

'How's it look?'

Ethan was sitting to the left of Johnny, who had eyes on the farmhouse with the binos. They were crouched behind some old weed-covered oil drums. They could see the farmhouse end-on, the front of the building facing out to their right. The side wall of the house was nothing more than an imposing stone wall, broken only by a black hole where a small first-floor window must have once been, and below it, a door hidden behind a pile of rusting trash.

'Like a farmhouse,' said Johnny. 'You know, roof, windows, cows in the bedroom.'

Ethan took the binos and had a look himself. The place was a wreck. Whatever life it had seen had left long ago.

Johnny said, 'If Luke and Nat had been here, we'd probably know the number of x-rays as well as Kat's location, but them getting caught has screwed the whole thing. We need to take a closer look before we work out what to do next.'

He slipped across the shadows and ducked in through the open door of one of the outbuildings at the rear of the farmhouse. On Johnny's signal, Ethan followed. The darkness inside the building felt thicker than outside, he thought. Ethan noticed that, although it was obvious the building hadn't been used in years, the faint smell of animals still lingered, trapped in the stonework of the walls.

Johnny pointed out through the door to the farmhouse. They could now see the rear of the house and the end wall they'd been able to see earlier. 'Light, ground floor. Flicker of one in a room upstairs too.'

'So where's Kat?'

Without taking his eyes from the farmhouse, Johnny said, 'I'm guessing upstairs, with the x-rays on the ground floor.'

A sound made Ethan look back towards where they'd come from. Then bright lights burst over them and they dropped to the ground.

'What the hell?'

'Don't move!' hissed Johnny. 'Whatever you do, don't bloody move!'

The sound of vehicle doors opening and shutting was replaced by footsteps crunching gravel. Ethan didn't breathe.

Johnny nodded at Ethan then risked a look through the door. Then he ducked back in and said, 'It's Nat and Luke. They're being taken into the farmhouse. At gunpoint.'

The lights died, everything went quiet.

'Too close,' breathed Johnny. 'They parked right where we've just come from!'

But Ethan wasn't listening; he was still replaying Johnny's last sentence.

'Sam said no one would be armed. You sure you saw right?'

'Totally,' said Johnny. 'An AK-47 has a very distinctive silhouette. Particularly when it's being jabbed into the back of a mate.'

Up until now, Ethan had been running on adrenaline and excitement. It was an exercise; they were all taking it seriously, and Sam was testing them. But to come up against this, to find that they were now facing weapons? That made him nervous.

Ethan raised himself to his knees to see a van, blue and beaten up, parked next to the oil drums. If they'd stayed there, the job would've been over before it had even begun.

'Nice of Sam to make things so interesting, isn't it?' said Johnny. 'Always our best interests at heart.'

'So not only have they got Luke and Nat, as well as Kat,' said Ethan, 'but they're also armed. How are we supposed to deal with that?'

'Like Sam said,' said Johnny, 'we adapt. So here's what we're going to do.'

Ethan leaned in. He was happy for Johnny to take the lead in this. Yes, he'd been with the team for a few months now, but in a situation like this, the best, safest thing to do was to follow, listen and learn.

'The whole point of what we do is that we're proper sneaky

bastards,' explained Johnny. 'And remember we've been taught by Sam, Mr Sneaky Bastard of the Year. So we're going to creep in there, head upstairs, grab Kat, Nat and Luke, then make sure our exit is clean.'

'We're going in just like that?'

'Just like that,' said Johnny. 'No time to hang around and have a meeting about it.'

Ethan was quiet, but couldn't help feeling that sometimes Johnny could do with reining in his just-do-it attitude.

'The x-rays are armed,' continued Johnny, now in full flow, 'and we need to avoid all contact. So silence is vital. The lights from the farmhouse are a good indication that the x-rays are downstairs.'

'How can you be sure?'

'Because that's what I'd do,' said Johnny. 'But that doesn't mean to say they won't be patrolling now and again, so we need to be careful and bloody quiet. We pile in there, we'll get our arses shot off.'

'No, we won't,' said Ethan. 'This is just an exercise. And aren't the x-rays Mal and Reg?'

Johnny turned to Ethan. 'A note to the wise,' he said, voice quiet, serious. 'If you don't treat this like it's the real deal, then when it is, you'll be slack, make mistakes. And if that happens, you're not just putting yourself in danger, but the rest of us as well.'

It was the first time Ethan had ever had Johnny speak to him like that. His instant reaction was to tell him to sod off, but he quickly realized Johnny was right. So he wound his neck in.

'OK?' said Johnny.

'Yeah,' said Ethan, and pushed all thoughts that this wasn't for real from his head.

'And just so you know, I've never seen the x-rays before,' said Johnny. 'I've a feeling Sam's called in a few more friends of his. Just to keep us on our toes. They look serious. And I doubt they'll hold back in giving us a good kicking if we just roll in there like none of this is real and it's all just a game.'

'Seriously?'

'You want to test it, go ahead,' said Johnny.

Ethan flicked a nod at his friend. 'You lead, I'll follow. That way, if you get caught, I can run for it.'

'You're learning quick.'

'You taught me well. So how do we get in?'

Johnny pointed to where the light was visible downstairs. 'I think there's a door just to the side of that window.'

'But that's right next to the x-rays. What if this is a setup?'

'Explain.'

'For all we know,' said Ethan, 'the lights are on in the farmhouse to draw us inside. Then, when we slip in, they spring the trap and we're in the shit because Kat, Luke and Nat are actually being held in another building.'

'But I saw Luke and Nat taken into the farm,' said Johnny.

'All they had to do was slip them out again,' said Ethan. 'I'm just saying we should be careful, that's all. Not just go in assuming we've sussed it right from the off.'

Johnny looked thoughtful for a moment. 'So what would you suggest?'

Ethan pointed at the other outbuildings around the house. 'First, we check those out. It'll only take a couple of minutes to do a recce.'

'And if all's clear?'

Ethan pointed at the end wall of the farmhouse. 'It's not much, I know, but that door has a stone lintel above it. If we can climb on that, I reckon it's big enough to take us both. Then it's a bit of a stretch to that hole where a window must've been, but I reckon we should be able to pull ourselves in.'

Johnny looked over at what Ethan was talking about. 'Doesn't exactly look easy.'

'Better than creeping past x-rays with AKs,' said Ethan. 'And if it doesn't work, if we can't reach, then we'll just do it like you said.'

Johnny frowned, then grinned. 'It's risky . . . dangerous. I like it!'

'Then let's get moving,' said Ethan. 'I'm seizing up, sitting here like a gnome.'

Johnny was up and off and Ethan was with him. They quickly checked the rest of the outbuildings and found them all empty. All their attention then turned to the farmhouse.

Back round at the wall they squeezed into the shadows and looked up. The aging, flaky brickwork was wet and slippery.

'Help me up,' said Johnny, nodding at the stone lintel above the door.

Ethan clasped his hands together, Johnny shoved in his boot and with a heave he had his hands on the lintel. Ethan pushed Johnny's feet as Johnny pulled with his arms. And he was up.

He then reached down to help Ethan up, pulling him by

one hand as Ethan grabbed onto the lintel with his other.

Now, both standing on the lintel, they looked up at the window above. Johnny went first, reaching to get a good hold, then walking his feet up the wall, finding cracks between the stone as best he could.

'Shit!'

Ethan instinctively turned away as Johnny held on to stop himself from crashing down. For a few seconds, he hung there, not moving. Then with a heave and a scrabbling of his feet, he was up and at last was through the window.

All the time Johnny was on the wall Ethan half expected to see someone come round the corner of the house. But no one did and, now inside, Johnny reached out, grabbed him and pulled him through and into the house.

The room was dark and smelled damp and rotten.

Johnny signalled to stick close to the walls and edge round to the door at the opposite side of the room. As they started moving, Ethan understood why; this way, they were walking where the floorboards had less flex than if they'd walked straight across the room. Their progress was quick and silent.

At the door, they both peered out onto a gloomy hallway. A light was visible coming up from the ground floor, dancing and flickering at the bottom of the stairs, which were directly in front of them. Across the hallway, a thin crack of yellow light slipped round the edge of a door.

Johnny pointed. Ethan nodded.

Sticking to the walls, they slipped out of the room. Ethan could now just make out the sound of a television downstairs interrupted by the occasional burst of laughter.

'Nice to know someone's enjoying themselves,' said Johnny, and peeked into the room. 'Bingo!'

Johnny opened the door and Ethan followed him in. Kat and Natalya were on the floor tied back-to-back. Luke was strapped to a chair.

Ethan went over to Luke as Johnny set to with the girls. They both used their hook knives and soon the rest of the team were all free. Ethan noticed that Luke was rubbing his wrists where the rope had cut into them; they were bleeding.

Johnny signalled to check everyone was OK.

Everyone nodded and Johnny led the way, slipping back out into the hallway, sticking to the walls as before.

With hardly a sound, they were soon all across the hall and in the room with the window where Ethan and Johnny had entered. But the sound of a door clicking open on the ground floor stopped them all dead. And they all then heard someone climbing the stairs.

Luke immediately turned to Natalya who, without a word, walked back to the door.

Ethan had no idea what was going on, but he was sure they should be getting out of the window, and fast, rather than hanging around.

Johnny pulled Ethan against the wall as they all tried to flatten themselves like shadows.

Natalya was at the door now. With a final look at the team, she coughed loudly. Ethan heard the person on the stairs stop for a moment, then start moving again, now heading directly for the room they were hiding in. He was confused. Why had Natalya given away their position? What was going on?

Eyes wide, heart thumping, Ethan watched as Natalya slunk away from the door and into the shadows herself. Then the door started to open and he saw the silhouette of a large man, pistol at the ready. A torch flicked on and a bright circle of light started to dance across the wall. It was moving towards them and Ethan knew it would be on them in a second.

Movement.

Ethan saw Natalya spring from the shadows at the intruder. In a blur, he saw her somehow grip the hand holding the pistol, twist it and ram it into the intruder's stomach. Before he even had a chance to respond, she was in at him with a punch that burst his nose. Before he had a chance to yell, Natalya broke the pistol from his hands. Luke came in from behind, grabbing the man round the neck, and leaned backwards, lifting his feet off the ground. The man struggled, but went still very quickly.

Ethan turned to ask Johnny what the hell had just happened, but Johnny hushed him before he had a chance.

'We need to move quickly and get the hell out of here,' he whispered.

In quick succession the team slipped from the room out through the window. With everyone on the ground, Ethan stood by Natalya.

'That was quite something,' he said. 'What you did up there – I've never seen anything like it.'

'It is called *Krav Maga*,' said Natalya. 'It was developed by the Israeli special forces. Effective, yes? One day I'll show you, Ethan.'

Ethan turned as he heard a noise behind him. It seemed

to come from the van that had brought Luke and Natalya to the farmhouse. Johnny stood there, holding up some cables.

'What are those?'

'Spark-plug wires,' grinned Johnny. 'These guys won't be going anywhere for a while.'

Kat said, 'Sam'll kill you, you know that, don't you?'

'I'm simply helping to secure our escape,' said Johnny. 'Can't have them chasing us in a vehicle, can we?'

With them all doing their best to keep their laughter down, the team headed off into the night. They were still smiling when they climbed into Sam's Defender twenty minutes later at the pick-up point.

'Went well then?' Sam asked.

Johnny slipped into the front seat and handed Sam the wires and winked. 'You could say that . . .'

8

'You broke his nose, Natalya! And when I say broke, you nearly smashed it off his sodding face! What the hell were you thinking?'

Ethan, like the rest of the team, was inside the tent and trying to stop himself yawning. They'd managed to get a few hours sleep after the exercise, but not enough. Sam was standing by a board leaned against the inside of the tent. It outlined their timetable for the day, starting at 0630. He looked as he always did, observed Ethan: hard and serious. Even though he knew Sam wasn't actually speaking to him, he still felt the heat of Sam's stare. And he was feeling more than a little awkward; it was clear that Sam had a problem with how the exercise had gone, but Ethan was having real problems seeing how else they could've gone about it.

'It was unfortunate,' said Natalya, and Ethan noticed how she sounded so cool and calm, despite being in Sam's firing line. Had he ever seen her riled at all? 'Unavoidable.'

Sam growled. 'What's the point of me training you to go in silent, to do the job and get out unnoticed if the instant I send you in you pummel someone?'

'We didn't have much choice,' said Kat, and Ethan could hear in her voice that she was restraining herself. Unlike Natalya, her emotions were much closer to the surface. 'If Natalya hadn't taken him down, and Luke knocked him out, then the other x-rays would've been on to us. It was clean and quiet. The others didn't have a clue until it was too late.'

Johnny backed her up. 'It had to be hard and fast, Sam. If we'd given that x-ray any chance at all, the op would've failed. And, as you've told us time and again, failure isn't an option.'

'And he was armed,' added Luke. 'We only had the element of surprise and we took full advantage of it. Natalya was the obvious choice, you know that.'

Silence.

OK, so they'd got the hostages out, thought Ethan, but it was clear that Sam felt they'd taken too many risks.

He said, 'I don't see how else we could've done it. I know Natalya went in hard, but—'

Sam cut him off. 'That's exactly my point. By going up against someone armed, you automatically put your life in jeopardy.'

'I still don't see what else she could've done,' said Ethan.

Sam drew himself up even taller; the man was a walking

70

wall. 'When you heard someone coming up the stairs, you stalled. You were too focused on dealing with him, rather than getting the hell away.'

'We didn't think there was time to get out,' said Kat.

'You hesitated,' Sam barked back. 'You switched focus, lost sight of the objective. The x-ray had to check the room you, Luke, Natalya had been held in. You had enough time to get out and scoot into the darkness, perhaps even time for Johnny to disable the van.'

The team went quiet. Ethan could see Sam's point now. He hadn't realized at the time, but they had taken a risk. What if it had been a real situation and the x-ray had managed to get a shot off? He didn't even want to think about the consequences.

Sam went quiet for a moment. At last, when Ethan felt like the silence would suffocate him, Sam said, 'None of you are expendable. And you are only as strong as each other. That's why the team works. Yes, you are all highly skilled, but one of the most important things for you to understand is what skills to utilize for whatever situation you find yourself in.'

The team were silent and Ethan could see that Sam's words had sunk in.

Sam visibly relaxed, dropping his hands to his side and slipping one into a pocket. 'Now we've got that over and done with,' he said, lifting the board and hanging it from one of the horizontal poles holding up the tent, 'this is the outline of how the next couple of days will run.'

Ethan, again, was impressed with Sam. He'd given them a bollocking, explained what they'd done wrong, then moved on. He didn't hold grudges.

'We're focusing on fitness and survival,' said Sam, 'interspersed with some skydiving. You're here to learn new skills, but not at the expense of those you've already got. And anyway, I don't want any of you to forget that when the skydiving competitions kick off in a few months time, I'm going to want to see some trophies.'

Ethan saw faint smiles slip onto the faces of the team. The fact that they were going to be skydiving as well as everything else was a great feeling; it was something they all understood and were not just good at, but addicted to.

Sam continued, 'Day starts at 0630 with physical training. Then eat, shower, and training proper starts at 0800. Lunch is 1230 to 1330. Then you work through till five in the afternoon. Skydiving will take place as and when the weather is decent enough. We'll be making good use of that helicopter to get you as up to speed with that as you are with leaping out of a plane. And you'll be on night tasks too. Clear?'

No one grumbled. Despite making a hash of the night exercise, the air had been cleared and they all knew what mistakes had been made. Now it was time to get on with whatever was going to be thrown at them next. And that, alongside the thought of skydiving, was enough to make Ethan smile.

From that moment on, each and every day worked the same. The team were up at 0615 for fitness training at 0630. It wasn't always a run. Sometimes Reg would vary it with shuttle runs, fifty-metre fireman lifts, press-ups, pull-ups and burpees. It made it more interesting, but no less hard to complete.

Ethan also soon knew how to build a shelter, purify water, some basic wild foods to scavenge, and how to kill and skin a rabbit. He learned about using smoke to signal to an aircraft overhead, how to carry out basic concealment, even using the stars to navigate. As Mal had explained, if he was in the process of effecting an escape, then he'd be moving at night to avoid capture, laying low during the day. Night navigation skills were vital.

But no matter what new skills he was learning, and how each one made Ethan feel further and further away from the person he had been only months ago, it was still the skydiving that grabbed him.

On the afternoon of their first day, Sam had taken the team to a field just away from their main site. In the middle of the field an area about the size of a couple of tennis courts had been measured out with tape pinned to the ground.

'Restricted DZ,' said Sam, turning to face the team. 'You're all used to landing in nice open spaces with plenty of room for error. Only Luke here has actually focused on precision landings. That's about to change.'

Ethan asked, 'How accurate do you need to be?' Looking at the area marked out on the ground, it didn't look exactly hard to miss.

Sam said but one word in answer: 'Very.'

Not more than half an hour later, Ethan was sitting with the rest of the team in the helicopter. The sound of the blades cutting the air just above their heads made conversation impossible, so all communication was by hand signals. Sam had just signalled that they'd be jumping in five minutes.

From the night before, Ethan knew how using a helicopter allowed a skydiver to be at least a little more accurate when getting eyes onto the DZ. What he didn't know was just how accurate he was able to be when coming in to land; his main focus had always been to land safely.

As they'd got themselves rigged up ready to go, Sam had explained that there would be a two-minute gap between jumps. This would allow each of them to focus on their own jump and accuracy, rather than where everyone else was in the sky.

Sam signed again; it was jump time.

Ethan watched as Luke slipped his feet over the edge of the door in the side of the helicopter. With a nod at the rest of the team, he was gone, almost like he'd been sucked out into the sky.

Waiting for Kat to go next, Ethan focused on everything he'd learned about skydiving, running through his exit drills in his mind, getting into a stable position, tracking . . .

Kat was gone.

Next it was Johnny. And he was taking this seriously. Ethan knew just how competitive Johnny was, despite his devil-may-care attitude. He'd be doing his all to nail this from the off.

Now it was Ethan's turn; Natalya would be coming in last.

He shuffled to the door, felt the wind suck his breath away. He swung his legs over the side and glanced at the ground below . . . thousands of feet below. It still gave him a thrill to be so high up, so precarious, and with only some material and cord to prevent him hitting the ground at over 120 mph.

Sam gave the signal.

Ethan was out. And it felt once again so different to jumping from a moving aircraft. Instead of having to deal with the speed he was already doing because of the forward momentum of the plane, now he just plummeted, face to the ground. He didn't tumble. Quickly springing into a stable position, his body rapidly accelerating to terminal velocity, Ethan scoured the ground for the DZ. When it came into view, it didn't exactly look as easy to hit as he'd first thought.

He checked his altimeter, adjusted his heading by tracking left, then did his best to maintain a steady, accurate descent for the DZ.

Despite knowing the air around him was clear, Ethan still did a 360-degree check before deploying his canopy.

It sprung from his back, pulling him to a slow descent in seconds. Once it was inflated, Ethan checked the lines for any tangles, made sure the canopy itself was fully inflated. Then he turned his attention to the DZ.

It felt great being in the air. This was something Ethan knew he was good at, and his confidence soared.

Using his steering lines, he kept himself on course for the DZ. Gliding down, it seemed as though it wasn't getting any bigger at all, almost as though he was being held stationary above it. Then the ground suddenly felt like it was rushing up towards him.

Ethan had been convinced he'd taken a good line, giving himself enough distance to swing round and glide in for a landing smack bang in the middle of the DZ.

But he was wrong.

The ground came up quick, Ethan pulled his steering lines

hard, killed his descent, but there was nothing he could do; he swooped straight over the DZ and landed softly in the field.

With Luke the only one who'd managed to land in the marked area, Sam had them all in the air again almost immediately. And Ethan could see Johnny wasn't happy; his drive for perfection to be the best damned skydiver in the world didn't seem to deal too well with not getting it right first time. Or having someone like Luke do better. He had a face on him like a slapped arse. Ethan worked hard not to smile; sometimes it was good to see that even the best didn't get it right all the time.

'Close enough isn't good enough,' Sam said. 'By the end of your time here, I expect you all to be landing accurately in an area a quarter of the size marked out now.'

At that moment, heading back for another jump, such a task seemed impossible to Ethan. But if he'd known a few months ago what he was about to get into, that would've all seemed impossible as well.

Climbing back on board the helicopter, Ethan set his mind to what Sam expected; and as far as he was concerned, that meant being able to touch down on a pinhead.

9

'EDI,' Sam said on the sixth day after a morning of more survival training. They were all in the briefing tent grabbing some food before the afternoon and some more jumps onto the restricted DZ. 'It's how we did things in the Regiment and how I do things here. Because it works.'

'EDI?' Ethan asked. 'What's EDI?'

Since arriving, Sam hadn't let up, pushing them day and night. At times Ethan had felt like he couldn't take in any more information. Exhausted at the end of each day, he'd do his best to chase over what he'd learned before shutting his body down for a few hours. He'd run through everything from how to light a fire and the best way to catch and dispatch a rabbit, to reviewing his daily skydives and working out how to improve on his accuracy. And it had improved, which was a good job really; Sam had cut the DZ area in half that day without warning.

'Explanation, demonstration, imitation,' said Sam. 'It doesn't matter if you've done something before; you can always improve on it. And that's the best way to deal with any situation. Doesn't matter how impossible or big something seems; break it down, start from the beginning, look at it in smaller chunks, you can deal with it.'

Ethan realized that this was exactly the process Sam had used for everything he'd taught them, as had Mal and Reg.

'My role is to teach you,' said Sam, 'to confirm you know what I've taught you, and then test you under stress before you go out on a job. Repetition is part of the game. The more you do something, the better you understand the parts it can be broken into, then the greater your chances of success.'

It made complete sense to Ethan. It also made him realize just how lucky he was. Sam wasn't going to let them miss anything; when he taught them something, he was doing it with the sole aim that they would be able to do it as well as he could.

'So with that sorted,' said Sam, 'I think it's about time we learned something new, don't you?'

Ethan, like the rest of the team, jumped at this. What was Sam planning now?

'Escape, evasion and interrogation,' said Sam. 'And I'll let Mal and Reg give you a proper briefing.'

Mal stepped forward. 'You're really going to love this,' he said.

Reg just smiled.

* * *

Some time later Ethan was in his tent crashed out on his sleeping bag, his brain aching from information overload. It was night time and the world was liquorice-black. Clouds had stolen the stars. When Reg and Mal had finished, the team had been sent back to get a last bit of rest before the exercise began for real. No exact details had been given on how long it would last, how many hours or days they could expect to have not only to survive outside, but also to get through the interrogation. And that, thought Ethan, was in itself unnerving. The only firm bit of information they'd been given was about how they would know when the interrogation was over. It would be a simple sign; if an interrogator wore a black armband, the exercise was over. Reg had explained that the sign needed to be simple and visual because, after what an interrogation would involve, they would all be disorientated and confused.

Ethan sat up. Again, he went through what Reg and Mal had told them. It didn't make him feel any better.

Mal had been brutally honest and Ethan had felt his respect for the man increase tenfold. And he remembered it pretty much word for word . . .

'First, accept you've been captured, which means you've got no physical control over what happens. Nothing, OK? You're in the shit. Deal with it. You'll be beaten up, cut, maybe even crippled, but there's nothing you can do about it. Instead, focus all your efforts on staying mentally alert.'

Ethan couldn't imagine what Mal had experienced. That he'd experienced anything like it at all was enough to give him pause for thought.

'Be the grey man and don't draw attention to yourself.

Avoid eye contact. Don't talk back or get aggressive. You'll survive longer.'

Ethan knew his temper could flare. He only had to think about the effect his dad had had on him over all those years – and how he'd spent so much of his time as a kid feeling angry. But since joining the Raiders, he'd gotten that under control. At least he hoped he had; he didn't fancy his chances with either Mal or Reg.

'They'll try to clobber you psychologically,' Mal had then explained. 'In the business we call this "fear up", where the interrogator tries to intimidate you, and "fear down" is where they try to make you think they want to help you. Stay focused, stay grey, don't co-operate.'

This had sounded like the whole good-cop, bad-cop approach.

'Zone out of what they're shouting at you or asking you. Get your mind onto something that really interests you, something that'll occupy it while the world around you feels like it's falling apart. That way, you've a chance of motivating yourself to get out; it reminds you of what you've got to live for.'

Then Mal had moved on to stress positions.

'A beating is effective,' he'd said, 'but nothing works as well as a stress position. Trust me on this. With a bag on your head, you're shut in a room filled with white noise, have water thrown on you to freeze you out, and then you're forced to stand so that every muscle in your body feels like it's going to snap in half. Exhaustion soon takes over. You have to stay focused and maintain your mental integrity, or you're screwed.'

'You need to hold out,' Mal had then said. 'You blab, your friends die. It's that simple. The Geneva Convention states the only information you should give – as civilians – is your name. Stick to it. The information in your head, no matter how insignificant you think it is, could cost someone their life. Remember that. And finally, if you want a way to keep your brain ticking over, plan your escape. Always look for an opportunity to get the hell out. It may be the only chance you have to stay alive. After all, once your interrogators think they're going to get nothing else out of you, what use are you? None. And that, people, means you're dead.'

Listening to what interrogation would actually involve, the reality of just how hellish it could be had shocked the team into silence. It was Kat who broke it, voicing not only her own concerns, but ones Ethan was beginning to feel too.

'Do we get any choice in this?' she asked. 'I know we all need to be ready for any eventuality, but this seems way out of our league.'

'How do you mean?' asked Reg.

'This is special-forces stuff,' said Kat. 'And I'm sure I'm not the only one here who's noticed that's not what we are. And if a job comes up where being captured and interrogated is a potential risk, shouldn't that be a warning light that it's actually not for us to do?'

Ethan noticed Natalya and Johnny nod a little in agreement. Luke seemed unmoved, was obviously drawing his own quiet conclusions. Ethan wasn't sure what to think, except that everything Mal and Reg had told them had been nothing short of terrifying. And the thought that he'd soon be going through it made him seriously question just what the hell he was doing there. Skydiving was one thing. Learning survival skills made sense. But no one had mentioned anything like this to them before. At that moment, it felt not just extreme, but as Kat was implying, completely beyond what they were being trained to do.

Before Mal or Reg were able to reply, Sam stepped forward. He folded his arms and stared at the team.

'As you all well know,' he said, his voice a low rumble, 'your absolute safety is my responsibility. A mission goes wrong, it is ultimately my fault. One of you gets injured, I am held responsible. You get sent into a situation that you find you can't cope with, then I haven't trained you right.'

'Then don't send us into a situation where there's a chance we're going to get snatched and interrogated,' snapped Kat.

Ethan could see a hint of concern on Natalya's face too, but as usual she and Luke were remaining silent. Kat, though, wasn't having any problems voicing her thoughts.

'This isn't simply about being able to deal with an interrogation,' said Sam. 'And you need to start seeing all of this training as more than just a simple set of skills. It's about your mind set, how everything you learn can affect everything else that you've been told or shown or experienced.'

'But interrogation?' said Kat.

'I will train you for all eventualities, no matter how remote,' said Sam. 'And the simple reason is because I want you all to have the best chance of surviving just about anything that can be thrown at you. And if that means scaring the hell out of you and forcing you to cope with situations most people would puke at the thought of, then so be it.

I'm not here to take it easy on you. I'm here to do everything I can to ensure you aren't just good – you're untouchable.'

Ethan saw Kat go to say something, then back down. He'd agreed with what she'd said, but hearing Sam's explanation also made sense. And even though the thought of going through what Reg and Mal had just explained made him want to quit simply out of fear, he knew now he wasn't going to. Not a chance of it.

Ethan sat up and shook himself to try and focus on what he'd feel like once the exercise was over. It didn't work.

A shout came from outside; Reg telling them all to be at the briefing tent in five.

Closing his eyes, Ethan did his best not to drown in the fear doing its best to swamp him and slipped out of his tent to join the others.

10

'Name?'

Ethan was on the ground, cold, wet and – even though he knew this was still an exercise – scared.

He said nothing, worked hard on being as grey as possible.

'Come on, kid, can't hurt to give me your name now, can it?'

Ethan bit down on his lip, drew blood. The metallic taste filled his mouth. He was kneeling in a puddle with a sack over his head, his hands tied behind his back. After giving his pursuers the slip for a few hours, his luck had eventually run out. He'd found the whole evading-capture thing exciting, like it was nothing more than glorified hide-and-seek. But from the moment he'd been caught, everything had taken on a sinister, threatening air. Telling himself it was just an exercise didn't make any difference; he was scared.

'Can't help you if you don't give me your name.'

Ethan knew his name was the only information he was allowed to give. Nothing else. Not a thing. But he wasn't going to give it yet.

A boot pushed Ethan in the back and without his hands free to stop him, he fell forward into the puddle.

Another voice joined the first. Ethan recognized neither. 'We haven't even started yet, boy. Ain't no one here to tell us when to stop, either. You hear me? While Daddy's away, we bastards will play.'

Ethan lay still. He could see nothing through the sack over his head. Whatever was coming, he couldn't control it. He had to accept that, just like Mal had said. So he did. He was shitting himself, but he wasn't going to give up. No way.

No one else spoke as Ethan felt himself lifted up onto his feet and dragged forward. He didn't struggle, didn't fight it, just let them take him, doing his best not to trip up.

Although he was blind, Ethan noticed changes. First the ground beneath his feet became smoother. Was it Tarmac? Concrete? Sounds changed. He was inside – he knew that by the echo of footsteps around him.

A door opened ahead. Then came a shove to his back. He stumbled forward, toppled to his knees, skidded, thumped down on his side. A door slammed shut behind him.

Silence.

Ethan was out of breath and in pain. He had no idea how long he had been on the run before getting caught. But he did know that most of it had been agony in no small thanks to the kit he'd been forced to wear; itchy jumper, ripped trousers, and a pair of crappy toe-crushing trainers. This was all to replicate being on the run in whatever clothes you'd managed to grab before your escape. And now he'd just had his first taste of interrogation. It hadn't been horrific, but that didn't matter. He'd been caught. He was alone. And no matter how many times he told himself it was just an exercise, tears came easily. What the hell had he got himself into?

Sound of a door opening.

'Time to play, shithead.'

Ethan didn't resist as once again he was pulled to his feet and dragged. He was as helpless as he was ever going to get. But he had to stay focused and push through the fug of exhaustion and fear threatening to suffocate his mind.

Ethan felt his hood ripped from his head. Bright lights burned his eyes and he blinked, couldn't open them properly. Eventually a desk grew in the light and behind it he saw a man with a smashed nose.

Crap, thought Ethan, recognizing him immediately as the x-ray Natalya had gone at back in the farmhouse. He knew then that things stood a better-than-average chance of getting more than a little bit rough. The thought of it churned his stomach; he felt helpless.

'Name.'

Ethan glanced as best he could round the rest of the room, if only to get some sense of where he was. He got nothing. No windows. Just grey walls, the desk, the ruined nose. And he'd already completely lost track of time.

FreeFall, his move into Johnny's flat? That seemed like another life completely. Perhaps because it was; how could what he was doing now have anything to do with normality?

An image of his mum and Jo flashed in his mind. He remembered the ruined flat. The fact that he wasn't there suddenly felt like a weight crushing in on his chest. He found himself questioning what he was doing, why he was away at all, when he should've been back with them, sorting stuff out, protecting them from his dad. What if the police hadn't caught him yet? What if he came back to the flat?

A voice bellowed in his ear, made it ring, smashed Ethan's thoughts of home into a thousand pieces.

'You deaf? Answer him!'

Maintain your mental integrity . . .

Mal's words were clear in Ethan's mind. He grabbed a hold of the image of his mum and Jo. This time, though, he focused on how he wasn't just here for himself, but for the three of them. He was going to make something of his life, show his waster dad exactly what he was capable of.

'Ethan Blake,' he said, but nothing else. And he made sure he kept his eyes low, staring into the middle distance. *Be the grey man . . .*

Then the shouting and yelling and insults began.

Though nothing physical, it was difficult to take. He was alone and didn't know how long the interrogation would last. It was psychological torture, he knew that. Calling him names, threatening him, his family, his friends, telling him that the rest of the team had broken down already . . .

'And what about your mum?' said the man with the smashed nose. 'You don't think we know about her? About your sister?'

Ethan felt himself go cold. What did they know about his family? What? He looked up.

'Ah, so we've hit a nerve, have we? Worried about your mummy, eh?'

Ethan couldn't help himself; he eyeballed the man speaking to him.

'Been some trouble at home, I see,' said the man. 'Something to do with your daddy?'

Ethan felt torn inside. What if his interrogators knew something he didn't? What if his dad had come home while he'd been away, and he'd just not been told? The list of what-ifs came at him machine-gun fast.

The man leaned in close. 'Just give up now, Ethan, and this can all be over. You can go home and everything will be just like it was.'

At that, Ethan pulled his eyes away. They were using his family against him, he realized. OK, so he had no idea what was going on in the outside world, but if he gave up now, he'd be failing not just himself, but his mum and Jo. And his dad would've won.

That wasn't going to happen. No way.

Ethan knew he *had* to survive this, and he remembered then what Mal had said about zoning out, focusing on something that would remind him of what he had to live for.

So Ethan buried down deep inside his own mind. And to keep himself as alert as he could, to block out what was happening, he turned his thoughts towards something he knew inside and out, something of such importance to his life he couldn't live without it: skydiving.

The sound of the shouting soon became background

interference to what Ethan was now remembering; his first ever skydive. Strapped to Sam in tandem, he'd been nervous and excited. Just thinking about it brought back the memory of the sensation of tasting adrenaline for the first time; the metallic taste in his mouth, a tingle in his fingers. His life had been in Sam's hands, and against all sense and logic he'd allowed the man to throw them both out of a perfectly good plane at 12,000 feet. It was a moment that had changed the course of his life for ever . . .

The hood was thrust back on. Ethan was pulled from his thoughts. This time the hood was used to drag him backwards out of the room. A door slammed behind him, another opened up ahead. A few steps later he was grabbed, spun round and his legs kicked apart. Rough hands forced him to lean forwards and he felt the rough brickwork of a wall under his hands, which were pulled high above his head.

Footsteps walking away.

In less than a minute, Ethan felt pins and needles prickling his hands.

Stress positions . . .

The prickling sensation soon spread down his arms and he felt himself starting to buckle. His left knee gave way and his foot shuffled forward.

A boot cracked against his ankle and pushed it back out to its original position. Hands pulled his arms straight. The prickling soon turned to pain.

Don't let them break you . . .

The pain became unbearable. He buckled again. A punch winded him, he was kicked and pulled back into position.

Then a shock of cold made him yell out as icy water was

poured over his head. It snatched his breath away; he gasped like a drowning man.

Ethan felt his legs give, but managed to catch himself before he hit the floor. It didn't matter. He was dragged back into the position again, shivering like crazy.

Seconds became minutes. Ethan lost track of time. Each time he was dragged back into the room with the interrogator, he was battered by more shouting. His interrogator would scream things which in a normal situation would make his blood boil. In this place, though, it was just words; he was numb to it. Numb to everything. The only thing in his mind was skydiving. It was his sole focus.

Remembering where he'd come from and how he'd got to where he now was, sent sparks firing and jumping through Ethan's brain. He pictured everything from clipping into a rig to dealing with a cut away.

His interrogator changed tack and placed a hot mug of tea and a fresh bacon sandwich in front of him.

'Come on, Ethan,' he said, gesturing towards the food and drink. 'These are yours, mate. Just tell me what I need to know.'

Ethan hadn't a clue what they needed to know. They'd never asked. Or if they had, he'd either not heard it or blocked it out. And he certainly wasn't their mate.

'The mission, Ethan, remember? Why did you HAHO onto that island a few months ago? What was all that about? Who were you working with?'

What? Why were they asking about that? Ethan was confused, caught off guard. He knew full well that the details of that mission were top-secret. Sam had made that absolutely clear.

'Smells good, doesn't it, the bacon? The tea's steaming hot. Warm you up good and proper. Just tell me about the mission, Eth. Come on; help me, I'll help you, right?'

Ethan's brain went crazy with flashbacks of the mission. He squeezed his eyes shut, forced his mind back onto skydiving. He wasn't going to give anything away.

The interrogator leaned forward and picked up the bacon sandwich.

'Last chance, Ethan. If you don't let me help you now, then I can't guarantee your safety. They've been taking it easy on you up till now.'

For the first time Ethan wanted to give up. The questions about the mission had thrown him. And smelling the sandwich made him realize just how hungry, cold and desperate he really was. But he just had to hang in there.

'No?'

Ethan stared at the wall and said his name, nothing else.

The interrogator bit into the sandwich, nodded at Ethan. He knew what was going to happen next.

It was the same routine again and again. But he didn't give in. No matter the questioning, he'd still stuck to just his name. He was in a little place in his mind, focusing not on the pain or the fear of being hit, but on skydiving, rehearsing moves in his head again and again and again.

After another bout of questions and shouting, his handlers went a step further than before. Rather than placing him immediately in a stress position, one of them stomach-punched him. When the interrogator spoke, Ethan felt his face close to his ear, could feel warm breath against his skin.

'I'm growing seriously tired of this, Ethan. Just give up, right? And if you think Sam's around to make sure we don't get too rough, you're wrong. You're alone, mate. We've got you for as long as we want.'

There it was again: *mate*. Hearing it spoken here made it sound like a threat.

Reeling from the punch, Ethan didn't have a chance to recover as he was snapped up straight, then kicked to the floor. He landed hard on his shoulder, pain stabbed him.

'Bastards . . .'

The word was out before he could prevent it.

'What did you say, Ethan?'

Ethan spat, tasted blood. Some sodding exercise this had turned out to be. They were going too far. He was exhausted, close to losing it. Where the hell was Sam, anyway?

Ethan felt himself grabbed and dragged to his feet. All thoughts of being the grey man disappeared. He'd had enough.

A voice came in close.

'You haven't the faintest idea just how much of a bastard I can be, Ethan.'

But Ethan wasn't listening. Not any more. With every ounce of strength he had left he launched his head backwards at the owner of the voice. He felt it make contact and heard the voice yell out. The hands let him go and the room was filled with screams.

Ethan's sense of payback was short-lived. He knew immediately he'd made a seriously big mistake. A boot crashed into his stomach with such force that he didn't just buckle, but felt his feet leave the floor. Then a heavy slap caught him across the side of his head, making his ear ring out and sting so hard it felt like it had been ripped off. He fell to his knees. Another slap against his other ear sent him to the floor and he cracked his head.

No chance to recover: hands grabbed him, the air filled with swearing, and he was back in the stress position, more icy water poured over his head.

Door slam.

Ethan knew he'd messed up, but how the hell anyone could be expected not to react under this kind of pressure, he didn't know. And anyway, how long had he been in there? Hours? Perhaps even days? How much longer were they going to keep him? What if he gave in – would it really matter? This was just an exercise, after all, wasn't it? It's not like giving up now would mean he'd find himself staring down at the bottom of a shallow trench, the barrel from a pistol pinching the back of his neck.

He was only human. He couldn't take it for much longer. He'd go insane!

The screech of the door opening hooked Ethan out of his thoughts.

'You lost it, Ethan.'

What? Questions in here? Why wasn't he being dragged into the other room? The voice was different too. Deeper.

'Failed, just like the rest.'

Ethan gave his name, tried to gather his thoughts. That voice. It sounded familiar. Maybe he was just making that bit up; wherever he was, the acoustics were weird, made every-thing sound strange.

'Shut it, Ethan. Give up. It's over.'

The hood was ripped off again. Ethan saw his new interrogator, realized why he'd recognized the voice: Sam.

'You blew it, Ethan,' said Sam, and any hope Ethan had of a little sympathy was blown to pieces in an instant. 'I thought I could rely on you. Seems that I was wrong. A pity. I thought you had potential. Guts. *Grit!*'

Ethan was in shock. What was Sam saying? That he was out? No longer one of the Raiders? No way! If he'd known his place on the team was at risk, he'd have focused harder. But what more could he have done?

'You've wasted my time, Ethan. No more chances. If you can't deal with this, how the hell do you expect me to be able to depend on you when the shit really starts to fly?'

Ethan muttered his name. It was all he could think to say. His mind was doing cartwheels trying to work out how he'd failed. Why?

'It's over! You screwed up once too often.'

Ethan said his name again, this time clearer, watched Sam turn away from him, head to the door. How the hell was this happening? Sam should've told him that his future with the Raiders was at stake. It wasn't bloody fair!

Sam turned back round. Ethan looked up, forgot all the stuff Mal had told him about not giving eye contact, being the grey man.

And then he saw it: the black armband.

Ethan knew it was important, couldn't remember why. He stared at it, searched for why he should know what it meant. Then he realized.

'It's over? The exercise?'

Sam nodded.

'Seriously?'

'Well done, Ethan. You look like shite by the way.'

'You mean I haven't been kicked off the team?'

Sam shook his head.

Ethan felt relief flood through him; the team was every-thing to him.

Sam walked over and stood in front of Ethan. 'But you know you screwed up, don't you? Reacting the way you did, slamming the back of your head into the interrogator; if this had been for real, you could have found yourself in a hole in the ground with a bullet in your head. Or worse. Understand?'

Ethan nodded.

'Let's get you cleaned up.'

Sam took hold of Ethan's arm and led him out of the room and down a corridor. At the other end, Ethan walked into a room where night time stared in through grimy windows barely covered by curtains like spider's webs. Here he found the rest of the team. And they were none of them in any better state than he.

Johnny walked over, helped Ethan to sit down at a battered wooden table. Wincing with aches and pains, Ethan couldn't hide from the only thought now in his mind; *had he lasted as long as the rest of the team*?

Sam handed him a mug of hot chocolate and a bacon sandwich. Then Kat rested a blanket rested over his shoulders.

'How are you feeling?' she asked.

'Like shit,' Ethan said. It felt good to see Kat again. He had a feeling that just hearing her voice could kick him out of a coma.

'If it's any consolation,' said Kat, 'you outlasted me.'

Ethan raised his eyebrows over the hot mug in his hands. He'd been in there longer than Kat? Well, that was something at least.

Johnny said, 'Looks like you've perfected the hundred-yard stare, anyway.'

Ethan nodded and gripped the mug even harder, felt the heat sting his palms, tried to force it down his arms into the rest of his body. He didn't care. It felt good. He took a sip, then another, and as the hot liquid slipped down it felt like it was bringing him back from the dead. Warmth spread through his body like fire through a tinder-dry forest.

Ethan turned to Sam and asked a question he wasn't sure he wanted to know the answer to. 'How long was I in for?'

'Forty-eight hours,' said Sam. 'Time flies.'

Ethan almost laughed, but at that moment another person entered the room and the laugh caught in his throat like cloth snagged on barbed wire.

It wasn't just the pukka suit that gave him away, or the action-man-neat blond hair. It was the way he entered the room with such self-assurance and self-confidence, like he assumed he was in control wherever he went.

It was the man from MI5: Gabe.

Ethan felt Johnny rest a hand on his shoulder.

'Looks like play time's over . . .'

11

An hour later, Ethan was cleaned up, fed, and despite being battered and exhausted, feeling a little more human. The rest of the team were also looking more like themselves, though Ethan could see bags under their eyes that looked black as coal.

They were back in the room with the cobweb curtains.

Gabe didn't stand on ceremony.

'Over the past six to twelve months, homeless teenage boys over the age of fifteen have been disappearing from the streets.'

'If they're homeless and presumably out of the system, how do you know?' asked Kat. 'And why would MI5 care?'

'Yes, people disappear,' Gabe answered sharply. 'It happens.

They fall off the radar, lose touch with their family and friends, with society. These kids were nothing more than a statistic. Little was thought of it. And no pattern in their disappearances was found because no one was out there looking for one.' He paused, then said, 'That was until one of them turned up looking like this.'

Sam passed around copies of a large colour photograph. Ethan looked down at it and saw someone about his own age. Only this guy was a complete mess. Cut, bruised and broken, he was lying on a hospital bed, a respirator strapped to his face, drips hanging out of him looking like his veins had been torn out. Whatever he'd been through, thought Ethan, it looked a whole lot worse than what the team had just experienced. And that was really saying something.

But then something struck Ethan as odd about the photograph, particularly with Gabe having just said that the boys who'd been disappearing were homeless.

'You sure he was homeless?' asked Ethan, not looking up from the photograph.

'Yes,' Gabe snapped.

'It's just he doesn't look it,' said Ethan.

'Trust me,' said Gabe. 'He was homeless.'

Ethan shrugged, but it still didn't sit right in his mind. If he was homeless, then why didn't he look all skinny and ill and malnourished? It wasn't like he'd have been getting three square meals a day, was it? And he'd have been living outside too, sheltering anywhere he could. His skin would be a mess. Everything about him would look battered and beaten and worn. But the boy in the photograph – despite being injured to hell – didn't just look fit: he looked like he'd spent every hour of the past however many months doing nothing but exercise. His body was lean and toned. Not massive and muscle-bound, but strong, solid. He was as fit as a butcher's dog. In no way at all did he look like he'd just come off the street.

'What happened to him?' asked Natalya. 'He was hit by a car to sustain these injuries, yes?'

Sam shook his head, and what he said next cut the moment with all the subtlety of an executioner's axe: 'He died two hours after that photograph was taken.'

The silence that slipped into the room at that news more than communicated the shock everyone felt at hearing it. Ethan stared again at the picture; the reality that the boy was dead sent him cold.

'However,' said Gabe, his voice calm, collected, 'despite his appalling injuries, we were able to get a few things from him before he died. It wasn't much, but it was enough to pique our interest. Which is where, I'm afraid to say, you all come in.'

'What about his family?' asked Kat, and Ethan not only saw raw emotion on her face, but also heard it in her voice. 'Do they know what happened to him? Have you contacted them?'

Gabe nodded. 'Of course. We have carried out all the usual procedures required in such a situation.'

'So you know why he was on the street, then? People don't just end up there for no good reason, do they—?'

'That was not our concern,' said Gabe, cutting Kat off before she asked another question. 'Neither is it yours.'

Ethan saw Kat clench her jaw, like she was physically forcing herself not to continue with her questions.

Gabe said, 'Our focus is on why he was snatched from the street. Not how he ended up there.'

Ethan looked again at the photo. Gabe's attitude sounded cold, unfeeling, and Ethan understood why Kat would find that difficult to deal with. Compared with the rest of the team, particularly Natalya, Kat was the one who didn't guard her thoughts; if something was on her mind then she said it. And now, with that photo in front of her, that's exactly what she was doing. Secretly Ethan wished he had the balls to do the same.

With another quick glance to Kat, who by now had turned her attention completely away from Gabe and back to the photograph, Ethan thought again about the boy who he now knew was dead. Whoever he had been – and 'boy' really didn't describe him at all – Ethan could tell that it was no car accident that had killed him. With injuries like that, Ethan hazarded a guess that he'd been battered, kicked till he was half-dead, then left for nature to do the rest.

He asked, 'Where did you find him?'

'Someone was walking their dog along a beach on the south coast,' answered Sam. 'Saw their dog sniffing at something. Found our boy here. Phoned the police.'

'That must've been awful,' said Kat, and Ethan again saw her face mirror just what she was feeling as she shook her head, closed her eyes for a moment.

'He was barely alive when they found him,' said Gabe. 'He regained consciousness twice, each time for no more than a few minutes.'

Luke asked the question on Ethan's lips. 'So if he wasn't smashed up in a car accident, what actually killed him?

How exactly did he get all those injuries? And what does it have to do with us?'

Ethan realized then he'd been too stunned by what he'd seen in the photograph to think why Gabe was here at all, telling them any of this. Luke had a point; what did this have to do with them? Why exactly was Gabe here?

Gabe sat back against a table, folded his arms. 'I'll cut to the chase. The injuries you see here are not, as Sam has already pointed out, from a car accident, or indeed from a simple beating. Our boy wasn't the victim of a mugging or a random attack by a bunch of drunks looking for some alternative entertainment after a night on the beers.'

'So what you're actually saying,' said Kat, her voice a mix of realization and distress, 'is that this wasn't just deliberate, it was planned.'

Gabe nodded and Ethan was impressed; Kat seemed to have worked it all out before the rest of them.

'So what was the reason?' continued Kat, like she was positively demanding answers from Gabe. 'Was it drugs, gang crime . . . what?'

'For a start, *planned* isn't quite the right word,' said Gabe, 'but the injuries are more than deliberate, that much is obvious. According to our pathologist, most of them match the type of injuries generally only sustained during a serious fight of what can only be described as ferocious brutality. And by that I don't mean one where he was jumped on or taken by surprise and had to fight back.' He held out an autopsy report and Ethan took it numbly.

Johnny said, 'You're not expecting us to believe he got these injuries in a fight he willingly took part in?'

The fact that Gabe didn't even nod made his silent confirmation of what Johnny had said even more shocking.

Sam said, 'He knew what he was doing and fought back just as hard. As shocking as that may sound, it's the only conclusion that can be drawn.'

Ethan looked at the photograph again, flicked through the autopsy report. He had to say something, particularly as no one else had as yet mentioned just how in shape the boy looked. 'Something else still isn't right.'

As he spoke, Kat said at the same time, 'He just doesn't look homeless.'

Ethan looked at Kat and in that brief moment knew they'd drawn the same conclusion. He nodded for her to say some more, but she shook her head, nodded back.

'Ethan?' said Gabe.

He glanced again at Kat, then said, 'Say you're right and he was homeless. If you ignore all those injuries, he doesn't exactly look like he's been surviving on the streets, does he?'

'Explain.'

'Maybe I'm wrong,' said Ethan, 'but I'm guessing if you're homeless, you don't have access to a gym.' He raised the photograph up to emphasize what he was saying. 'Whereas he has a body you only get if you train for hours every week and sort your diet out. This is someone who's lived on protein shakes, not stuff nicked out of wheelie bins.'

Ethan sat back, pleased to have finally got that off his chest. Out of the corner of his eye, he was sure he noticed a faint smile on Kat's face. He didn't respond; it was just nice to know that they were on the same wavelength.

Gabe nodded and looked again at the files in his hands.

'For your information,' he said, 'his injuries include cracked ribs, broken teeth, split lips, smashed nose, swollen eyes. He has bruises that match those sustained from punching and kicking. He has a fractured bone in his leg and his knuckles are heavily bruised. And that's just the fresh injuries you can all see here. His body is quite literally covered in older injuries, badly healed fractures, scars.'

'Add to that zero body fat, huge lung capacity, serious muscle mass,' said Sam, 'and I think you all know where this is going.'

'But you can't be homeless and keep fit,' said Johnny.

'Traces of steroids were also found in his blood,' said Sam, ignoring Johnny's comment. 'His diet seems to have been focused completely on peak performance: high protein, slow-release carbs, dietary supplements like creatine. In a word, all the stuff you'd expect to find in someone training hard for something. And by training, I mean doing little else but.'

Kat spoke for them all: 'Like what, Sam? What exactly was he training for?'

Gabe explained. 'With the information you have in front of you now, and looking not just at his injuries, but his diet, his physiology . . . it all matches that of a professional fighter.'

'Not a boxer, though,' said Sam. 'But a cage fighter. Someone used to being in a ring where anything goes.'

'Kids cage fighting?' said Luke, and Ethan heard the usually unwavering voice shake a little in disbelief. 'That's impossible, Sam. Cage fighting may be completely insane, but it's mostly legit, so long as you're over eighteen. And the blokes who do it are all mixed-martial-arts experts. People get hurt – but they don't usually die.'

'All we're doing is giving you the facts,' said Sam. 'And they tell us that this kid died not because he was beaten up by accident, not because he was hit by a pissed-up loser behind the wheel, but because he was fighting on a regular basis and got unlucky. Sounds crazy, I know, but there is no other conclusion. Trust me, we've tried to find one.'

Ethan thought back to what Luke had said earlier, and when he spoke next he had a feeling he was asking the question on everyone's mind. 'So why are you telling us? Just what the hell happened to him and what's it got to do with us?'

Sam closed the file he was holding, pulled out a chair and sat down. He leaned forward, rested his elbows on his knees and looked at the team. 'As Gabe mentioned, before the lad died we were able to get a little information from him about what he'd been through, how he'd ended up in such a state and washed up on a beach. So what we're telling you isn't simply based on what we learned from what you've just seen. It's also because of what he told us.'

'He told you he was a cage fighter?' said Kat, and Ethan heard disbelief in her voice.

Sam said, 'Yes. He wasn't very coherent, and he kept falling in and out of consciousness, but from what he told us, what we now know is that he was kidnapped off the streets. No warning, nothing. Just snatched. A professional abduction with no witnesses, no evidence, nothing.'

'How?' asked Luke.

'Not sure,' Sam replied. 'The lad remembered only that he was taken and ended up in a place with a number of others like him. All of them homeless.'

'I'm beginning to wish I wasn't listening to this,' said Kat, and Ethan saw her turn the photograph face down on her knee, like she'd had enough and that was the end of her involvement. He was half tempted to follow suit.

'It gets worse,' said Sam. 'From what he told us, we think that this is a highly organized operation involving the kidnapping of homeless lads, just like him, to be trained up and forced to fight in illegal, high-stakes cage fighting.'

Sam allowed what he'd just said to sink in. Then he spoke again. 'Whatever happened in the fight, we can only assume that he lost. And losing obviously came with a heavy price; he was probably dumped out at sea and left for dead. He had a bullet graze on the right of his head – someone wanted him dead, but fouled the shot, probably figured he'd die anyway and didn't go in with another to make sure. Somehow, he managed to get to shore, but his injuries, and the exposure he suffered, were too much for him to cope with and his body shut down.'

Gabe pulled a laptop computer from a bag on a table nearby. He opened it, switched it on and inserted a disc. A picture flickered into focus on the screen. 'Just watch,' he said.

Everyone fell silent.

12

Ethan wanted to turn away, but ghoulish fascination took hold. He couldn't help but watch what was happening on the screen, no matter how wrong, how violent.

Two lads, both around his age, one in red shorts, the other blue, were shut in a hexagonal cage at least two metres high. They were circling each other. Both were bleeding. The one in red had only one eye working, his other was swollen so badly it looked like a lump of fresh, bleeding meat. His arm was covered in blood from trying to wipe it clear. The rest of his face wasn't in that much better shape and his knuckles, held up as they were to try and protect his head from any further damage, were cut and bloody.

The one in the blue shorts looked in an even worse state,

dragging his right foot behind him, his left arm hanging uselessly. Ethan guessed it was broken. Either that or so severely dislocated that he could do nothing with it. Blood was streaming from the side of his head and down his body from a torn ear.

Ethan turned away from what was on the screen and saw that the rest of the team were all equally horrified. Johnny's usual carefree demeanour had been replaced by a stare both hard and unwavering. Luke looked the same, though whereas Johnny had leaned forward, his hands clasped together white-knuckle tight, Luke was leaning back in his chair, arms folded. Ethan wasn't sure if Natalya was looking at the screen at all, but her eyes were narrowed, her lips pursed. Of all of them though, it seemed that Kat was the most affected. She was visibly horrified, and Ethan was for a moment taken aback by just how affected by it she was; there were tears in her eyes, but at the same time she was refusing to turn away, almost as though she was forcing herself to fully understand what the boy in the photograph had been through.

Ethan turned his attention back to the screen. The fight was becoming even more brutal. 'Look, I think we get the picture,' he said, concerned now about how the film was affecting the team. 'We don't need to see any more. We can guess the rest.'

'No,' said Gabe. 'You have to see this. You need to understand exactly why we need you and what you are going to be up against.'

Looking again at the violence on the screen of Gabe's computer, Ethan wondered just how many times Gabe and

Sam had watched what he and the rest of the team were all seeing now for the first time. Then another thought struck him; *for people to put money on a fight like this, then others must have watched it live at the time.* He had no idea how many; it was a chilling thought that sent him so cold he felt almost dizzy with it. Nausea swept through him. And he saw Kat turn white.

When the fight finished and the screen went blank, Gabe broke the shocked silence. 'We believe,' he said, 'that the boy found on the beach is just one of God knows how many kids to have ended up like this.'

'You mean dead?' snapped Kat. 'Why the hell did you have to show us that? We could've guessed what happened!'

'We believe,' said Gabe evenly, 'that the whole show is being run by an arms dealer, known to us only at the moment as "Mr X", who we've been trying to catch for years. He runs an operation smuggling weapons into the UK, and we have no idea where or how. We are, to say the least, desperate to nail the bastard.'

Ethan was impressed with how Gabe managed to stay unfazed by what he was saying, or by the reaction of the team, particularly Kat. He wasn't being cold, Ethan knew that; he was being professional.

'We have never been able to collect enough evidence to bring him down,' continued Gabe. 'However, if we can find a way into this cage-fighting syndicate, we think we have our best chance at not only apprehending him, but also exposing those he deals with: serious criminals, terrorists – you get the picture.' Gabe nodded back towards his now-dead laptop. 'This is the kind of game that attracts big earners with questionable moral compasses. Just the kind of punters our Mr X likes to deal with.

'Wherever these fights take place and are filmed – and it could even be offshore – the likelihood is there will be a server to relay the recording to all of the people who are signed up to watch. Certainly Mr X will want to make sure the relay only goes through a secure and isolated server rather than through any other more traceable hardware.'

Things were suddenly getting technical, thought Ethan, and he doubled his effort to listen in and take note of every detail.

Gabe continued: 'If we can get to the server, we can get to Mr X's customer list. And with that kind of information in our hands we could radically improve the security of this country and its people.'

Despite Gabe's sudden patriotic turn, Ethan could see what he was getting at. Information like that which he had described would be priceless.

Natalya said, 'So we kill two birds with one stone: the intel on this contact list will take you closer to Mr X, and we save the lives of the boys fighting in cages, yes?'

'Your job is to get the intel,' said Gabe. 'As for rescuing anyone, that's already taken care of. Once you've completed your job, UKSF are to be sent in. They have already been briefed accordingly.'

'UKSF?' asked Ethan.

'United Kingdom Special Forces,' said Luke. 'General term to cover the SAS and SBS.'

'Hang on, Gabe,' said Johnny. 'There's something I don't really understand. How did you get in there to pick the boy up first? How come you guys got to him before the police, particularly as it was them who got the phone call from the poor sod who found that boy in the photograph? That doesn't make any sense. What is it you're not telling us?'

Ethan saw Gabe glance at Sam.

'Told you they'd want to know everything,' said Sam. 'That's why I picked them. Don't miss a thing. You're going to have to tell them. They should know, anyway.'

Gabe looked back at the team. 'He was working for one of my other teams, undercover, living as a homeless kid, doing a grey op to try and gather intel on a drugs ring, trace suppliers. It had nothing at all to do with the cage-fighting operation at all. It was just luck that we stumbled on this.'

'Not exactly lucky for him though, was it?' said Johnny.

Ethan was astonished by Gabe's revelation, and judging by the silence that followed Johnny's comment, it was obvious that the rest of the team felt the same way. But what really hit home for Ethan was that whoever the boy was, he'd been doing the same kind of work they had all been trained for. His cover story was probably different – something worlds apart from skydiving – but it was the same world; he been sent in to do a job for Gabe, something no one else was qualified or suitable for. And it had gone wrong. Horribly, catastrophically wrong. And now he was dead.

Gabe spoke. 'One moment he was there; the next moment he'd gone,' he said, his voice quieter. 'We lost all trace of him. He just vanished. Then, some months later, details of a lad matching his description being found on a beach flashed up on our system.'

Ethan saw Kat look up at Gabe. 'How could you let this

happen? To go undercover he must've trusted you, Gabe. What happened? Why didn't you look after him better?'

'We did, to the best of our abilities,' said Gabe.

Kat bit back with, 'Well, it doesn't exactly make me feel safe. You going to allow the same thing to happen to us? Are we as expendable?'

'I never said he was expendable.'

'What else are we to think? He's dead, Gabe, for God's sake!'

Sam raised a hand. Kat fell quiet, though Ethan could see she was finding it hard to hold back.

'Right,' said Sam. 'Listen up and listen good. Everything you've heard is top-secret. The reason you're being called in on this is because I think you're Gabe's best chance of nailing the bastard responsible. And that means not just stopping more lads disappearing and getting kicked to death, but putting a serious hole in the illegal arms trade. So let's tell you a bit more about the mysterious Mr X.'

Gabe said, 'The reason we call him Mr X is because that's what he calls himself. His real name is unknown. He seems to like the air of mystery it gives him. It's also a little theatrical.'

'And Mr X likes a bit of theatre,' added Sam. 'His trade-mark is the black cane he carries, topped with a silver ball. He's in his fifties, about my height, and as English as Earl Grey tea. But that's really about all we know as regards looks. What photographs we do have of him are blurred at best. He's kept himself hidden from prying eyes for years, is an expert at it.'

'And that's because he pays serious cash for the best in

the business,' said Sam. 'The man has his own private army to protect him and to run his operations. The people he employs are all ex-forces, mercenaries. Serious customers who know what they're doing and are very, very good at it. Take him, for example.'

He handed out a photograph of a man walking down a nondescript street. Although solidly built and – if you looked closely – with what appeared to be a few scars on his face, he didn't stand out.

'Ex-Israeli special forces. Kicked out for gross misconduct. Disappeared soon after. Now he works for our man. He's a weapons specialist, which ties in well with the arms dealing. He's also an expert in CQC – close quarter combat – a *Krav Maga* expert and general all-round nasty bastard. Which makes us think he's probably got something to do with the cage fighting.'

Luke asked, 'How long has the cage fighting been going on? Do you know how many others have been killed?'

'In all honesty,' said Gabe, 'we haven't a clue. We didn't even know about it until our boy turned up on the beach. Could be months, could be years.'

'Either way,' said Sam, 'we need to bring it down as soon as we can.'

'We get this Mr X,' continued Gabe, 'the effect will be global. Do not underestimate the importance of bringing him down.'

'If you need any more convincing,' said Sam, and he picked up the photograph of the lad who'd been washed up on the beach, 'think on this: he's no different to any of you. He was selected, just like all of you here, because he had particular skills that made him suitable for jobs few others could do. He's paid the ultimate price. You owe it to him to find out what happened and help bring down those responsible.'

Once more, Ethan found a question pushing itself to the front of his mind. 'OK,' he said. 'But why us, and what exactly is it you're asking us to do?'

13

'This is what's going to happen,' said Gabe, and the team all leaned in to listen.

Ethan noticed the atmosphere in the room change. No longer were the team simply being given information. They were now involved; their full attention was now with Gabe and Sam.

'Of the team, only Ethan and Johnny match the profile of those being snatched.'

'So no girls have been taken?' asked Natalya.

'On the information we've so far collected, no, and the boys taken are all young, younger than Luke,' said Gabe.

Ethan felt a tap on his shoulder and found Johnny with a coin in his hand.

'Flip for it?'

The coin went skyward, but Sam caught it before it hit the deck.

'It's you, Johnny. Ethan's still too new to all this. You've had a lot more training. It's that simple.'

'Why not a professional soldier?' asked Natalya.

'Because a professional soldier would stand out,' said Sam, 'particularly one of the right age. He wouldn't pass for a homeless kid; too smart, too fit. A trooper from the Regiment would be too old. Anyone else would look awkward, unconvincing. You have to trust my judgement.'

Ethan watched Johnny sit back in his chair, obviously accepting what Sam had said.

'And this,' said Gabe, 'is how it's going to happen. Johnny will go undercover as a homeless teenager,' he explained. 'We know the area our boy was snatched from very well, as he'd been working the streets there for some time. And we've identified that a number of others around his age have also disappeared from the same place in the past year. Which is chilling, to say the least.'

'So my aim is to be snatched deliberately, right?' said Johnny, sounding a little disbelieving. 'Which means you want me to agree to be put in a position where I'm at risk of ending up like your boy in the photograph.'

'That sounds like suicide,' said Kat.

Gabe's face didn't flicker any degree of emotion. 'It's the only way for us to get in. We'll have proper surveillance. You will be fitted with a tracking device in your teeth: completely undetectable. We're not going to lose you, I promise.'

At that moment, Kat said, 'Did you say the same to the boy in the picture?'

Ethan expected Gabe to respond, but instead all he did was send a quick flick of his eyes at Kat then continue with his explanation.

'Assuming this pays off and you do get snatched, Johnny,' he said, 'the rest of the team will follow, pinpoint the location, effect a covert entry, find the server, grab the intel on the arms deals and contacts, extract the undercover operator, then get the hell out.'

'Why not UKSF?' asked Ethan. 'Wouldn't they be better at the extraction?'

He understood the reason for sending one of them in undercover as they'd blend in better than a trained soldier, but what was the point of sending them all in as follow-up?

'Because not only are we able to drop you into very inaccessible places – which we think this might be – but your very existence is, to be frank, above top-secret,' said Gabe. 'What you do is known only to a handful of people. We cannot allow knowledge of who you are and what you do to get out. The repercussions could be severe.'

'And this is what you're trained for; this is exactly the sort of covert operation where we need to operate more or less invisibly,' said Sam.

'So we do all this before the cavalry arrives,' said Johnny. 'Just like that?'

'Yes,' said Gabe. 'Just like that. And as soon as we know the intel is out and you're clear, we send in UKSF. They'll deal with freeing the boys who've been abducted, and will apprehend any x-rays. We did think about not sending the rest of the team in, just having Johnny pulled out with the rest of the abductees. But the risk, we think, is too high. There's a chance the evidence could be destroyed in the process or the intel not found. Better to manage it ourselves before extreme force is used.'

'And let's not forget,' said Sam, 'that the point of this op is that you're all involved in making sure that you, Johnny, don't end up in that cage. Understood?'

Johnny nodded.

'Good,' said Sam. 'Now, as I'm sure you all know, for an op like this, I'd usually want at least three weeks in the hangar for build-up training. Not just to revise the skills you've already got, but to do the specifics, the skills-to-task required to do what's being asked of you on this job.'

'Hangar?' asked Ethan. 'You mean we'll be training for this back at FreeFall?' He didn't think that was a great idea; surely it would be next to impossible to keep their preparation for the job separate from what FreeFall was actually all about: skydiving as a leisure activity.

Sam said, 'Hangar's a generic term, Ethan. It basically means anywhere we go to isolate a team for build-up training. Most times it is a hangar – somewhere large enough for a team to live in and do their training, shut off from the outside world. There's an area near Hereford the Regiment use for this kind of stuff.'

'So where are *we* going?' asked Kat.

'It's a secure location close to where Gabe's lad was snatched. The camp you've been at until now has already been stripped. Everything's been prepared for your arrival.'

'Sounds like you assumed we'd just say yes and agree to do the job,' said Johnny.

'No,' said Sam. 'I expect you to do as you're told.'

'So how long have we got?' asked Luke. 'Or do we not want to know?'

'Five days,' said Sam, 'and then Johnny will be going out on the street. And you all need to be clear by that point on exactly what you're doing. Or before you know it, he'll be dead.'

The team were taken by helicopter from where Gabe had briefed them to the so-called hangar. The hangar was all function, no style. Its location wasn't on any map.

Sam gave Johnny his cover story so that he could get used to it well enough for it to become second nature when he finally went operational, and he was ordered to refrain from washing and to stay in the same clothes from that point on. As Sam had explained, for Johnny to convince as a boy living on the street he had to look and smell the part; deodorant and a close shave were a dead giveaway. Much to everyone's relief, Johnny was given his own room.

The next day started very early as Sam first debriefed each of the team in turn on the interrogation training exercise they'd just completed. Luke was already drinking tea at the kitchen table when Ethan returned from his debriefing. 'How'd it go?' asked Luke.

'OK, I guess,' Ethan said. 'But I thought I'd totally messed up. I did what Mal told us, but I still reacted.'

'I heard,' said Luke. 'But we all broke down in our own way.'

Ethan was amazed to hear this; he'd thought he was the

only one who'd lost the plot. 'What happened to you?'

'Well, I didn't nut one of the interrogators' – Luke smiled – 'though I wish I had.'

Ethan laughed.

'Anyway,' said Luke, 'you shouldn't be so hard on yourself, Ethan. The point of the exercise is that we're broken; it forces us to look at ourselves differently, to understand better our own frailties. The exercise only ends when you finally crack.'

Ethan sat up at this. 'You mean we had to fail to pass? That's brutal!'

'It's not, actually,' said Luke. 'Should any of us be in that situation for real we'll know not just what to expect, but why we cracked during the exercise. That way, there's less chance of us giving up should the worst ever happen.'

Luke stood up to stretch then turned back to Ethan and said, 'Just so you know, you lasted longer than any of us. Something to be proud of, that.'

As soon as the rest of the team had completed their debriefing, Sam moved on to the job in hand.

They gathered round a kind of street map. Except on this one Ethan saw no street names and it had been cut into four sections, like quarters of a very badly baked pie, and colour-coded clockwise green, yellow, red and blue. Every road junction had a number.

'This,' said Sam, as Ethan tried to understand what he was looking at, or what use it could be, 'is the area of streets and alleys Johnny will be working.'

'But where are the street names?' asked Ethan. 'How are we supposed to know where any of us are if we're out following him?'

'Street names are a pain in the arse,' said Sam. 'Colours and numbers are clearer and easier to learn and understand.'

Ethan knew he didn't look convinced.

'It's simple, really,' said Sam. 'You all need to know this map off by heart. If you have road names to remember, it would take you for ever to get it right. And, when I call through and tell you to go from say Red One to Yellow Three, you'll all know what I'm talking about.'

He went on, 'We'll be using dead letter drops, or DLBs.' He then pointed at four of the numbered junctions, one in each coloured quarter of the map, and handed out photographs, all showing a bin next to a bench at four different locations. 'Johnny, if you've left something at a DLB, you'll make a mark on one of these bins, OK?'

'So we won't be using live drops?' asked Luke.

Sam shook his head. 'We want to avoid the risk of actually meeting in person and compromising the op.'

Sam handed out a further four photographs. 'These are the actual DLBs,' he said. Each photograph showed a location Johnny could access with little trouble, one of which was a hole in a tree down an alley.

Luke asked, 'Is that a DLB or where Johnny will be dossing down?'

Johnny didn't laugh quite as enthusiastically as the rest of the team.

'As Johnny's going to be wearing a tracking device,' said Sam, 'we're not going to have you lot following him night and day. Doesn't matter how good you think you are at tracking someone without getting pinged, if you're seen regularly in an area, it could arouse suspicion. We don't know who we're dealing with here. They could be monitoring the area more than we know and we can't risk it.'

'So what will we be doing?' asked Natalya.

'Natalya, I need you to put Johnny through some serious training for a start,' said Sam. 'Time for you to pass on some of your *Krav Maga* expertise. I've brought out dummy weapons for you. He's got plenty of CQC experience, but I want his skills honed for obvious reasons.'

'Just in case of what?' asked Johnny, even though they all knew the answer.

'Worst-case scenario; we always prepare for it,' said Sam. 'If you get snatched and we lose you for a while, you could end up wherever these kids have been taken without any backup, at least until we trace you again. We don't want you there with no way of protecting yourself.'

'With my training you will be OK,' said Natalya. 'You will be well-prepared!'

Ethan saw in that calm face of hers a fire suddenly flare in her eyes. She looked so slight, yet after what he'd seen back at the farmhouse during that first exercise he knew she could quite literally punch above her weight.

'And the rest of us?' asked Luke. 'I'm assuming we're not here simply to make the tea.'

'Assuming Johnny gets snatched and we trace him to the cage-fighting operation, Kat is going to be the one to sort the intel and not only download everything Gabe's after from the server, but screw the system with whatever virus we can get hold of. She's always the one to trust if there's anything to do with computers.'

Ethan said to Kat, 'So you're a computer geek as well as a world-class skydiver? I never knew that!'

'Not so much a geek,' said Kat. 'I'm that rare thing: a chick who digs PlayStations.'

'And both Luke and Kat will be responsible for keeping tabs on Johnny here at base,' said Sam. 'The tracking device he'll have in his tooth will send an encrypted signal via satellite to our equipment here. We'll be able to pinpoint him to within a few metres, which is pretty good. All of you will take it in turns and do planned – but randomly timed – sweeps of where Johnny is, keeping an eye on the DLBs just in case.'

'What about me, Sam?' said Ethan. 'What else do you want me to do?'

'You're Johnny's backup,' said Sam. 'Like an understudy in a play, you have to learn your own cover story and Natalya will give you a crash course in CQC and *Krav Maga*. You'll be a good sparring partner for Johnny. That way, if Johnny is compromised and we pull him from the op, you're on. Right?' Sam glanced over to Natalya. 'They're all yours. You've got three days, then I need them ready for the street.'

14

Briefing over, Ethan was outside with Johnny and Natalya. All he knew of *Krav Maga* was what he'd seen from Natalya, and that had resulted in a splattered nose; he was looking forward to learning a fighting style so effective. He wasn't so keen on the idea of being a sparring partner though.

'Johnny has some knowledge of *Krav Maga* already,' said Natalya to Ethan. 'It is an Israeli martial art developed during the persecution of the Jews in Germany and is based on street fighting. It is designed to be effective against the use of clubs, bottles, knives and firearms.'

Ethan had never before heard of *Krav Maga*; he wondered what made it so special? 'What about other martial arts like karate or jujitsu?' he asked.

'Complicated and ineffective,' dismissed Natalya. 'Krav Maga is instinctive. It trains you to use simpler, basic moves; punch, kick, bite, gouge. It is brutal. So, we warm up, yes?'

Ethan quickly learned that what Natalya actually meant was to push yourself close to exhaustion. Through a series of runs, punching and kicking drills and other exercises like press-ups and burpees, she had both him and Johnny soon gasping for air.

No sooner had the warm-up finished than Natalya was moving them on to basic fighting drills. With a nod, she handed Johnny a dummy pistol made of black rubber. He thrust it in her back.

'Always keep your hands at waist height,' she said, her eyes on Ethan. 'It is more difficult for the attacker to see what you are doing. And you must look for execution triggers, something that tells you you're likely to be shot.'

'Like this?' said Johnny; jabbing the pistol in Natalya's back, he started to yell at her to get on her knees. And he sounded like he meant it; for all his joking around, Ethan could see that getting on the wrong side of Johnny would be a bad idea.

Natalya reacted, flipping round to the outside of the arm holding the pistol. Gripping Johnny's arm against her body with her right arm, she went at his neck with three succes-sive blows from her free elbow, then brought her foot down into Johnny's leg, forcing him to the ground. Finally she broke the weapon from Johnny's hand and slammed it down onto his face, still holding his arm. Johnny dropped.

Ethan was speechless.

'Survival is not just about defence,' said Natalya, helping

Johnny to his feet. 'First principle of *Krav Maga* – as with any form of martial art – is to *avoid* a fight whenever possible. If that means giving someone your wallet or the keys to your car, you do it. Always walk away if you can. But if that is not possible, then you must attack your attacker.'

'Isn't that still asking for trouble?'

Natalya shook her head. 'You will live longer if you know how to neutralize the threat and make sure your attacker is in no fit state to chase after you to do further damage.'

'And that means using everything around you,' said Johnny. 'A wall or a tree . . . a table. It does not matter; just use it to your advantage.'

Ethan asked, 'Why didn't you use the pistol on Johnny once you had it?'

'Most weapons on the street are either replicas, do not work, or the person holding it does not know how to use the safety,' explained Natalya. 'Much better to use it as a club and break their face open.'

Now it was Ethan's turn. He was given the rubber pistol and told to keep his finger out of the trigger guard.

'It is why we call disarming moves *breaks*,' said Natalya. 'They usually snap the finger holding the trigger.'

Ethan jabbed the pistol in Natalya's back. A blur of movement was all he noticed and Natalya had him disarmed and on the floor. He hadn't stood a chance.

'Now you try,' said Natalya.

After running through the drill a few times, Natalya put the pistol away and worked Ethan and Johnny through some unarmed basics, deflecting punches and kicks and dealing with an attack from behind.

Johnny grabbed Ethan round the neck, forcing him to bend forward. Following Natalya's instructions, Ethan looked up at Johnny and brought his hands to gouge his face and grab the arm round his neck. He then twisted out of the hold, kept a grip on Johnny's arm and sent his foot into his stomach. Johnny dropped to the floor.

'I think you're getting the hang of this,' he said.

Day five came round so quickly that Ethan half felt like he'd been kicked out of a dream. Sam had everyone in the dining room at the house. By now it was feeling almost like home and Ethan was pretty comfortable. Kat poured the tea.

'Seriously,' said Johnny, 'tea's just not doing it for me any more. It's turning my skin a funny colour.'

Sam ignored him. 'Let's run through what we're all doing,' he said. 'We'll start with the mission statement.'

Sam handed a piece of paper around with a simple sentence written on it. Ethan had no idea what Sam was on about.

'This is how it's done in the Regiment, and it's how we're going to do it here,' Sam explained. 'It feels stupid, but we all read it twice out loud, OK? That way we all understand why we're here and what the ultimate goal of what we're doing actually is.'

Sam was right, thought Ethan; that did sound stupid. But he wasn't about to say so. As one, the group read aloud what was on the paper: *The mission is to stop the dealing of arms by Mr X.*

Once they'd read it twice, Kat came in with, 'But I thought we were going in to bust this cage-fighting thing? Isn't that what this is all about?'

Sam shook his head. 'That's all part of it, but not the ultimate goal. Stopping the cage fighting is a lucky bonus. You're here to find out where the fighting takes place and get to that server. Gabe and his cronies are convinced it is kept in the same place. I cannot emphasize enough the impact of this mission being successful.'

'You make it sound like the boys doing the fighting don't matter,' said Kat.

Ethan heard the edge in Kat's voice again. It was becoming clear to him that she wasn't in this just because skydiving made her sexy – which it seriously did – but because she really wanted not just to do something with her life, but to do something that mattered. He liked that a lot.

'I'm going to forget you said that, Kat,' said Sam, and he turned to Johnny. 'It's late morning now. I want you on the streets by 1400. The sooner you're on the street, the better for us. You smell terrible.'

'You're to blame for that,' said Johnny. 'All that bloody *Krav Maga* stuff and not being able to shower.'

'No more talk,' said Sam. 'We go live in an hour. Johnny, how's the tracker device in your tooth?'

Ethan hadn't seen it being fitted. It had happened a couple of days ago; someone grey and nondescript had turned up at the house, spent half an hour with Johnny, then left.

'Fine,' said Johnny. 'Feels like I've got a toffee stuck in it, but I reckon it's secure.'

'The signal is crystal,' said Luke. 'Tracking will not be a problem.'

Sam turned to Ethan and Natalya. 'I want you two on the ground when we let Johnny go operational. You'll do a four-hour rotation. I'll be with you so we all do four on, eight off. It'll keep us fresh, give us time to sleep and keep sharp. You're not there to stop him getting snatched. You're there as rapid reaction backup if he finds himself in trouble. The homeless are easy pickings for idiots and drunks out for a bit of meat.'

'Such a way with words, Sam,' said Johnny.

Sam went straight on with his orders. 'Johnny, you'll be dropped off at a location that will allow you to move out into the sector we've got mapped without being noticed. It would be pretty weird if we just dropped you off in a shopping centre in the state you're in. You'll have blankets, a tobacco tin, and a sleeping bag which, incidentally, may look rotten, but is a military-spec arctic bag that'll have you cozy down to minus forty, so you should be fine.'

'What about a dog?' asked Natalya. 'Is that also not part of the uniform?'

Sam stood up. 'Get to it everyone. Now.'

A couple of hours later Ethan was looking at Johnny through the window of Sam's Defender. They were parked round the back of an old warehouse. It was a serious fall from grace. Johnny looked not just homeless, but half-insane, with his usually well-styled long blond hair sticking out like the hair of a wet cat.

Sam leaned over Ethan to speak to Johnny. 'This is all a massive long shot, Johnny, but we've just got to go with it. No matter what, we're right behind you.'

Sam pulled the Defender away and Ethan watched Johnny's reflection shrink in the wing mirror. He wouldn't say it out loud, but he was pleased it wasn't him.

15

Ethan was sitting in a 24/7 café. He was starting to think that if he had to do another four hours waiting around for nothing to happen he might go insane. Opposite was the alleyway Johnny had called home for the past three nights. Ethan had a good viewpoint of anyone going in or coming out. It was a dead end anyway, so at least no one could come at Johnny from behind.

It was close to midnight and the streets were filling up with boozeheads all out to see if they could find somewhere else that stayed open even longer. A girl in a minidress stumbled against the window Ethan was staring through. She giggled, blew him a kiss, fell away. Watching her leave, half wishing he was out trashing himself like everyone else, he spotted a group of three blokes on the other side of the road. They were hanging around the entrance to Johnny's alleyway. Ethan wasn't sure, but they looked like they were shouting at something down it. Probably a dog, he thought.

Then they moved into the alleyway, leaving the main road behind.

Ethan knew something was wrong. These weren't the guys come to snatch Johnny, that much was for sure. This was no organized street abduction; it was the beer talking everyone up to a tough walk, a lot of shouting and a chance of some easy, risk-free violence.

Ethan called it in.

'Keep an eye,' said Sam. 'It might be nothing. Stay clear, but keep me updated.'

'Want me to go help?'

'Negative,' said Sam. 'Do not blow Johnny's cover.'

Ethan knew he needed to get a closer look though. Downing his tea, which had gone cold a long time ago, he shuffled out of the café and into the night. As he strolled down the street, then crossed over, the cold bit hard, snapping at his skin like it was trying to pull it off in little pieces.

The men were further down the alleyway, and they were still shouting. Ethan couldn't make out any words, but they were definitely shouting at something. Or someone.

Over the road now, Ethan did a sweep of the alleyway, doing a walk past as though going somewhere else, glancing down to get a quick look. And what he saw confirmed his worst fears; Johnny was about to be on the wrong end of a serious kicking. The three men were towering over him as he lay in his sleeping bag, trying to get some shelter from the weather by squeezing in close under a skip filled with trash.

Ethan called it in. 'Sam, he's about to be beaten up.'

'Positive?'

'Totally,' said Ethan. 'Three pissheads and not a brain between the lot of them. Definitely pushing him for a fight. Any minute now they're going to drag him to his feet and give him a serious hammering.'

'You sure this isn't what we've been waiting for; Johnny getting taken?'

'They're drunk, Sam,' said Ethan. 'No transport in sight. This is just three blokes cruising for a fight. Against three, Johnny doesn't stand much of a chance, even with what Natalya's taught him. He'll be knackered, cold and not in any state to take care of himself and get the hell out.'

No word from Sam. Then, 'OK. Get in there. Now, before it's too late. But remember, see if you can sort it without resorting to violence first.'

Ethan gritted his teeth and turned back. A shout echoed through the alley as cats scooted out as if their tails were on fire. Ethan saw one of the three men reach down and drag Johnny up from where he'd been lying. Johnny was playing it calm, being non-compliant, as grey as he could be. Then the one holding him grabbed him round the neck as another went in with a kick to his stomach.

Before Ethan could even break into a sprint, Johnny was on the offensive. Blocking the kick, he pushed back against the man who had him round the neck. Ethan saw Johnny's hand shoot up into the man's face three times, slamming his jaw shut to smash his teeth, then breaking his nose. In the confusion, Johnny twisted himself out of the arm round his

131

neck and wrenched it hard, bringing his free arm down with such violence that Ethan knew the man's arm was broken. Before the other two could react, Johnny threw the now almost-unconscious man who'd attacked him at his two mates. He stumbled and fell at their feet. Then Johnny turned and legged it, speeding out of the alleyway and not even seeing Ethan.

With a last look down the alleyway to make sure the three blokes weren't about to go on the hunt for the homeless guy who'd just taken the fight to them, Ethan turned and followed after Johnny. He made damned sure it didn't look like he was trying to catch him up.

Eventually, just ahead, Ethan saw Johnny nip into a shuttered shop entrance, graffiti all over the door and walls.

Ethan didn't stop. Instead he did a walk past and called in to Sam. 'I was right,' he said. 'They were cruising for a fight.'

'Johnny OK?'

'Yes,' Ethan replied. 'Gave them the shock of their life thanks to that *Krav Maga* stuff, then bolted.'

'Where are they now?'

'Nowhere in sight,' said Ethan, turning and walking back past Johnny, trying to make it look like he was phoning for a taxi and walking to keep warm. But on his second pass, he noticed something. Johnny was crouched down, holding his arm awkwardly, clearly in pain. 'Sam? I think Johnny's bust his arm.'

'Broken?'

'Can't say,' said Ethan. 'Couldn't see exactly. But he's definitely in pain. He needs immediate extraction.'

Sam was quiet, then he came back with, 'Right, this is how we'll do it. If I come to you, our cover's totalled. So make it look like you've noticed Johnny's hurt and you've gone to help him.'

'Then what?'

'Walk him out of there and get him to Yellow Four. I'll be outside the closed-down bingo hall.'

'OK,' said Ethan, and Sam was gone.

Ethan turned to Johnny, conscious that he should look surprised and concerned, as though he was just being a good Samaritan.

'Hey; you OK? What happened?'

'Eth!' Johnny hissed through clenched teeth, but Ethan cut him off with a shake of his head.

'Stick with the cover,' he whispered. 'Remember we don't know each other, right?'

Johnny nodded and cut the volume in his voice, making sure no one would be able to see him speaking to Ethan, ducking down further into the shadows. 'Where did you come from? I didn't see you.'

'I was across the street,' Ethan explained, seeing the pain clearly on Johnny's face and checking him over. 'I saw the blokes come at you.'

Johnny said, 'They were pissed up. It wasn't a snatch, I knew that straightaway. I tried to do the whole avoid-confrontation thing, go grey, but didn't have much choice. My wrist's shagged.'

'Can you stand?'

'I said it was my wrist, not my foot,' said Johnny and got to his feet.

'Well, lean on me anyway,' said Ethan. 'It'll look good.'

Johnny did just that. Then Ethan led him to where Sam was waiting. But all the way there he had a bad feeling about this; with Johnny out of action, he was up next.

'Sorry, mate,' said Johnny, and Ethan could tell he was having trouble not laughing, 'but we've not got time for you to get all ripe and stinking. So it's my clothes and no alternative.'

It was early morning and everyone had managed to grab a bit of kip. Ethan was outside, breakfast eaten, and looking down at what Johnny had stripped out of when they'd got him back after his brawl in the alley. His friend's wrist was now in bandages and a sling. It was only a sprain, but it still meant Johnny was out of action for a while until he could move it again. And he was showered, clean and wearing clothes that didn't stink like a dead badger. That honour was about to pass to Ethan, who wasn't exactly relishing the idea of being Johnny's replacement.

'How did you put up with smelling like that?' Ethan asked, pushing at the pile of clothes with his foot.

'You get used to it,' said Johnny. 'Don't think of it as a smell, think of it as a process of maturation. Like cheese.'

'Do I seriously have to put it all on now?'

Johnny shook his head. 'You're on the street tonight. You don't need to put them on until you're on the off.'

'Lads!'

They turned to see Sam standing in the door to the house.

'Burn everything but the jacket, the larger pair of trousers and the jumper, and get them up on a line or something to give them at least a bit of an airing. That lot will go over what you're wearing today, OK, Ethan?'

'Yeah, Sam. Then what?'

'Someone's coming in at 1500 to sort you a tracker out like Johnny's. You'll leave at 1700.'

16

A further three days and nights in and Ethan was beginning to think that despite all the preparation, the job was a dead end. Sam had told him he'd be out for five nights before they'd call him in and review. Ethan was finding it hard to see the point of waiting out the other two days. All that had happened was Johnny getting mugged and injured and himself being sent in as a replacement. There was no sign of any kind of abducting going on at all. And he was half tempted to get to one of the as yet unused DLBs to tell Sam to call it off.

Ethan knew he stank. He could do nothing about it. He hadn't had a wash since he'd last been at the hangar. Despite his best efforts, his clothes were damp, his sleeping bag was damp; the closest he got to tidying himself up was to drag his sorry arse to the nearest public toilets. But the soap dispensers were empty and he wondered if going there actually made him smell worse.

At least he wasn't hungry. He'd followed Johnny's advice on where to scavenge for food. The large bins out the back of a posh supermarket just five minutes away from where he was kipped down had proved to be a godsend. The food wasn't even out of date most times. Cold, maybe, but it kept his belly full. He'd even managed to maintain a pretty balanced diet, what with the amount of fruit and water he'd found, as well as all the cold pies, meat and sandwiches he'd scoffed his way through. The only problem Ethan had with eating was that it made him very aware of the tracker in his teeth. It was supposed to be pretty much impossible to spot, but ever since it had been fitted Ethan had been more than a little aware of it. Getting him out on this job to replace Johnny had felt rushed from the off; the last thing he needed was to be worried that the tracker had been put in badly.

He finished off the crayfish, mayonnaise and salad baguette he'd found the night before and washed it down with a carton of cranberry and raspberry juice. He couldn't avoid the fact that he wanted this all to be over. In a few hours, day three would become day four. How long was Sam expecting him to stay out here? It sucked. Big time.

Ethan pushed the last of the baguette down his neck, swallowed, took a gulp of the juice. He'd managed to find some scraps of old carpet to lie on, and had fashioned a shelter out of a few large cardboard boxes, waterproofed a little here and there with strips of plastic he guessed must've been used for wrapping deliveries to the supermarket. But it was hardly luxury. Each night had brought with it disturbance after disturbance. If it wasn't a drunk taking a slash, then it was a cat or a dog or, as it was the night before, a fox that had tried to get in to nick his stash of food.

Ethan stuffed himself as deep as he could into his sleeping bag, made sure as little of the outside world as possible was visible through the makeshift shelter and closed his eyes. Two more nights, that's all he had to put up with. He could do it; he had to. He'd need his energy so any sleep he got was a blessing. At the very least, it made the time go quicker than sitting, staring into the middle distance, dreaming of hot showers, skydiving and Nancy's bacon butties. And all of that was definitely worth the wait.

Ethan was close to drifting off when he heard a vehicle turn down the alley in which he'd made his home. He wondered for a moment what shop around here would take a delivery so late, decided that was possibly the most uninteresting thought ever to breach his mind and got back to going to sleep.

The sound of the vehicle's engine grew louder; it was getting closer.

Ethan opened his eyes. The vehicle was directly outside his shelter. He heard the swish of a van door opening, then footsteps.

Ethan's breath caught in his throat like a hairball. He lay still, trying not to make a sound. Who was out there? What did they want? If it was the police, surely they'd have called him by now . . .

Then Ethan's world collapsed in on him. The shelter

crumpled and he felt like he was about to be crushed. Rough hands grabbed him, hauled him out. His struggling was pointless; he was still in his sleeping bag, hadn't a chance. He caught sight of faces in the dark as he was manhandled towards the open side door of a van. Ethan went to shout out, but a hard slap across his face stung him quiet, filled his head with stars. He was airborne for a split second, then landed heavily inside the van.

Dazed from the slap, he saw two men climb in after him, the last pulling the van door shut. Finally the van reversed, turned, and Ethan felt it shoot forward. He rolled helplessly across the floor, cracking his face on the side of the van.

Blood.

The sharp, metallic taste of it in his mouth helped bring Ethan to his senses. Wherever he was going, and whoever had him, he'd find out soon enough. The team would have him on the tracker in his teeth. They'd already be following him, of that he was sure. Now, though, he had to survive. And that meant he had to focus on his training and find out as much as he could without giving anything away: be the grey man.

The van swung left, the speed causing Ethan to roll. He felt a boot stop him and shove him back. He closed his eyes to focus on what he could hear, but nothing gave him a hint as to who his kidnappers were or what they wanted. If these were the people they had been looking for, the gang abducting teenage boys for the cage fighting that Gabe had told them about, then they were certainly efficient. He'd had no warning, been snatched so quickly he was helpless. And now he was completely at their mercy, trapped in his sleeping bag. It was unnerving as hell. At least he knew he had backup. He didn't want to think what this must've felt like for all those who had already been taken, who had no idea where they were going, or why.

'Sam? *Sam!*'

Luke's voice shook the house. The team had got used to nothing happening, so the sound of the urgency in his voice shook them from whatever they were doing. They all bounded into where Luke was sitting with the tracking kit; Sam was first in.

'What's up, Luke? What's happening?'

Johnny, who'd been eyes on Ethan, was on the line; Luke handed his earphones to Sam.

'It's worked!' Johnny hissed. 'Ethan's just been bundled into the back of a white van.'

'You get the plate?'

'Yeah; Luke has it.'

Sam looked to Luke who nodded and said, 'The tracker's working fine. Ethan's definitely on the move, and at speed.'

Sam said down the phone, 'Johnny, stay put. We'll come and get you when we're satisfied we know where Ethan's gone.' He killed the phone. 'Is the rest of the kit ready?'

Natalya said, 'Yes; everything we need: clothing, electronic lock gun and everything else is packed and ready to go.'

'Excellent,' said Sam. 'Now, everyone into the Defender!'

Back in the van Ethan could feel every lump and bump in the road. Which was why, after a sudden turn to the left, he noticed the terrain change dramatically; no longer was it the occasional pothole – it felt like they were speeding down a farm track. Ethan did his best to protect himself from too many knocks and bumps and was relieved when, a couple of minutes later, the van stopped. But then he was dragged out and dumped on the ground.

Ethan remembered his cover; whoever these men were, they had to believe he was fearing for his life; if he was too calm, it would look odd. So he rolled around on the ground, yelled out, screamed: 'Get off me! Who the hell are you? What do you want? *Help!*'

Between panicked shouts, Ethan blinked away the dark and could make out trees in moonlight. Four men were standing just away from him in the gloom, completely unfazed by his outburst. He sat up, pulled himself out of his sleeping bag; if they were going to attack him, he didn't want to be stuck inside it when the kicks and blows came.

He caught movement behind the four men. There was another with them, someone keeping to the shadows.

A voice broke the silence and it came from that someone: 'Soften him up a bit.'

Ethan didn't like the sound of that at all.

The voice continued: 'Let's see what he's got, hey, boys?'

It wasn't much, but it was enough to convince Ethan he'd struck gold: these guys had to be connected to the cage fighting. Despite the situation he had now found himself in, Ethan was almost relieved; the job was at last turning out to be a success. If he kept his head, and the rest of the team did their job, it would soon all be over.

Footsteps, then an arm gripped him round the neck, twisting his head down to face height.

Gasping for breath, Ethan tasted adrenaline. Judging by what he'd just heard, he figured if he didn't at the very least fight back, these guys were going to mash him up real good. But neither did he want to make it look too rehearsed, show them he knew what he was doing. He wasn't an expert in *Krav Maga* quite yet – that would take a lot longer than a few days – but he knew enough to put someone out of action. He needed these guys to see a fighter in him, however, not someone with skills.

Principle one of what Natalya had taught him about *Krav Maga* had already been compromised: no way was this going to be something he could just walk away from minus his wallet. If he was going to stand a chance at all he was going to have to fight back. It would have to look desperate.

Ethan felt the arm round his neck tightening as he was dragged forward. He looked about, saw a tree coming up fast. He needed to move before it was used to give him a headache.

Ethan twisted to look up at the bearded face of the man who had him. He wanted to slam three sharp jabs with his open palm into the man's chin, but that would look suspicious and could easily break the man's face open. That would be bad; he'd be pissed, his mates angry and then Ethan would be on the receiving end of something a whole lot more serious. Ignoring his urge to drive the man's chin out through the top of his head, Ethan started to yell again, try to pull away. He heard the man laugh and that angered him. But how was he going to keep himself protected without just going for it?

The man stopped, squeezed harder. With a yell, Ethan

stamped hard on the man's feet, then slammed a clenched fist into his bollocks.

The arm round his neck slackened, gave way, as the man howled. And over the howls, Ethan heard laughter. Lots of it; they were obviously finding it funny that the apparent bum they'd just picked up was a fighter and was giving their mate a hard time.

Ethan slipped from the man's arm, backed away, gasped for breath. He yelled out 'Help!' again, even though he knew no one would hear. It had gone beyond good acting. He would have been hard-pressed to stop himself yelling in the circumstances anyway. He saw the other men circle, cut him off, stop him backing off too far and disappearing into the dark. He made to shout again, but a hard backhand caught him full on across his face. His skin stinging, he stumbled to the ground, his hands only just stopping him eating dirt. More blood was in his mouth. Ethan spat to clear it, felt something hard flick through his lips.

'Shit . . .'

Lying in the mud was the tracker device from his teeth. Ethan was seriously annoyed with himself now. From the moment the thing had been put in it had never felt right; why the hell hadn't he said something, told Sam? Not much he could do about it now. More of a worry was what would happen if his attackers found it; he knew he'd be as good as dead. But without it, he was no better off. Crap.

Ethan caught sight of a kick coming for his stomach, grabbed the tracker at the last moment, tensed up for the hit. When it connected he was lifted off the ground and nearly threw up when he came back down.

Pushing himself to his feet, trying to clear his head to deal with whatever was going to come next, a thought struck Ethan; the tracker, even if it was still working, was already completely useless. He couldn't hide it anywhere. And if it was found on him, his attackers would know something was up, the cover would be blown. He'd be dead.

Shit . . .

The man Ethan had punched in the bollocks was still doubled over, moaning. He was hoping now that he hadn't done too much damage, otherwise his survival would be seriously compromised. The other three, though, now looked like they were seriously spoiling for a fight. Ethan knew he had to continue with the job and do whatever he could to make it work. He had to adapt.

Pretending to brush his hands against his trousers, Ethan made himself look as pathetic as he could. He stumbled backwards and, in the same movement, dropped the tracker to the floor. He crushed it good and hard under his foot, making sure it was buried deep in the mud. Then he fell to the floor and started to beg for mercy, his voice all but a whimper. Inside, he felt like an absolute tit, but he was also scared; even if he did fight back, one against three were shoddy odds. He'd maybe get in some damage to one or two of them, but they'd still have the advantage. He was completely alone now. All that mattered was survival; he needed time to work out what to do next.

Two men came for Ethan at once. One grabbed him round the neck and the other came in with his feet. Ethan managed to dodge the kick enough to have it glance off his leg rather than crush his stomach, but it still hurt and he yelled in pain.

A voice called out from the shadows. 'Enough!'

Ethan's chest was heaving; he hadn't realized just how out of breath he actually was. He looked up and saw the man who'd kicked him was pointing a pistol directly at him.

The voice came again. 'You're going to be rather entertaining.'

Next, Ethan heard a sharp blast of air and something jabbed into his leg. Reaching down, he felt a small dart jutting out.

Then the world went black.

17

'That isn't right . . .'

Sam didn't take his eyes off the road ahead. 'What isn't?'

'Well,' said Luke, staring at the equipment he was using to keep trace of Ethan, 'Ethan's tracker device has stopped moving.'

'That's a good thing, surely?' said Kat from the back of the Defender. 'Means we're getting close, right?'

Luke shook his head. 'The area's just woodland. It doesn't look like the kind of place you'd be able to hide a complex big enough to run this cage-fighting thing without someone discovering it.'

'Perhaps the woodland has to hide only the entrance?' said Natalya, who was with Kat in the back. 'Could it be underground?'

'I suppose,' said Luke. 'But that would involve either building such a place – which would be pretty damned obvious – or finding that such a place already existed. And that's impossible because where the tracker says Ethan now is; well, it's ancient woodland, not some new bit of evergreen forest.'

'So what are you saying?' asked Kat. 'That this doesn't look right? Does that mean Ethan's in danger?'

'Kat, we don't jump to conclusions, you know that,' said Sam. 'We just need to get there and sneak in for a quick look-see, OK?'

'Take the next left, about half a mile,' said Luke.

'How far then?'

'Not very far at all,' replied Luke. 'I suggest we park up immediately and someone goes to have a nosy.'

'Ready, Natalya?' asked Sam, standing beside the Defender where it was now hidden, deep in some thick bushes.

'Yes, Sam. As always.'

With that, they slipped into the dark, leaving Luke and Kat to stare at the faint, unmoving signal being given out by Ethan's tracker.

When they returned, Kat was the first to speak. 'Where's Ethan? What's happened?'

Natalya climbed back into the rear of the Defender and Sam pulled himself back in the driver's seat, squeezing Kat up close to Luke.

'Sam?' Kat asked again. 'Where's Ethan? What's going on?'

Silently Sam reached out his hand, opened it. 'Ethan's

tracking device,' he said as Kat and Luke stared at the small metal thing resting in his palm. 'That's why it was stationary; he was no longer wearing it.'

Kat said, 'But that means—'

'It means nothing,' said Sam, his voice low like thunder. 'It must've been knocked out. There were signs of a scuffle on the ground where we found it. Looks like they pulled down this lane to rough Ethan up a bit, try him out. Probably wanted to see if he was up to scratch.'

'So we don't actually know where he is at all?' Kat was starting to sound more than a little concerned.

'He was here, that much we do know,' said Sam. 'We found fresh tyre tracks going in and out.'

'What use is that?' snapped Kat. 'For all we know Ethan's had the crap beaten out of him. Maybe he's even dead!'

Sam clenched his fist then woke up the Defender. Its engine roared into the night like a chainsaw attacking the dark. 'Luke?'

'Yes, Sam?'

'Punch a call to Johnny. Fill him in with what's happened. Tell him we're on our way to pick him up.'

Kat, her voice strained, asked, 'And what about Ethan?'

Sam pulled the Defender from its hiding place, swung it onto the track. 'Until we know otherwise, we assume the positive, that he's alive and now on his way to wherever the cage fighting takes place.'

'So he's on his own? Oh, that's just great! And how exactly are we going to find him now? All we've got is a number plate . . .'

Sam didn't say a word.

* * *

Ethan woke to yet more darkness and the sound of others talking. The world was moving, the floor beneath him rumbling. His hands were tied behind his back; he could feel a strip of plastic digging into his skin, slicing into his flesh. Not that it hurt; the thing was so tight it had done a good job of cutting off his circulation. These guys really knew what they were doing. They didn't use rope, waste time with knots; they used plastic tags.

Doing his best not to give away the fact he was now conscious, Ethan eased his eyes open to a slit. He was back in the van, which explained all the movement. Opposite him were two of the men who he'd recently fought with. He couldn't make out any features in the shadow. It was them he'd heard talking. So he stayed lying as still as he could and listened in.

'Hurts, then?'

'Kills. He's a fighter, at least. None of the others have ever tried to crush my balls.'

'Lucky shot or are you just getting old?'

'Sod off!'

So, thought Ethan, *it's the one with the beard.* He had to force himself not to smile at the fact he'd done this bloke enough damage to have him still complaining about it.

'Only asking.'

'For a minute there it was like he knew what he was doing,' said another voice. 'He looked up at you like he was thinking what he should do next.'

'Let's just hope he brings in some serious cash before breaking his neck.'

Ethan felt his stomach churn. He really had done every-thing he could to make them see him as just another Joe from the street. All he'd done was punch the bloke between the legs. He seriously hoped that whatever suspicions they were voicing now would soon be forgotten.

He zoned out of the conversation. He'd heard enough, but any elation he felt at having done his job well enough to get snatched by the right people was suffocated by the fact that his tracker was lost, ground deep into the mud where the men had attacked him. The team would have no idea where he was or where he was going. He was alone and up to his neck in the deepest shit he could imagine. But he wasn't about to give up. Sam hadn't chosen him because he was the kind of person to roll over as soon as things got tough. Hadn't that interrogation exercise taught him that, at least? His only chance of getting out alive and completing the mission was to stay alert. Or he'd sooner or later find himself washed up almost dead on a beach himself. Or in the belly of the deep blue sea.

Ethan shut everything out of his mind so he could focus on where he was now and what was going on around him. He needed to pick up as much intel as he could. Because he wasn't just going to do his best to survive and escape; he was going to make sure that if he did get out of here in one piece, he'd have enough in his head to go back to Sam and send the team in to finish the job.

The van slowed. Ethan could hear water. He had no idea how long he'd been unconscious. Were they by a river or the sea? Sniffing the air, he tried to catch even a hint of the coast in it, of seaweed and ozone, but all he got was fuel fumes as the van door was swished violently open.

Cold air rushed in and Ethan felt the shock of it make him shiver as he was picked up and dragged out by rough hands. They knocked him about roughly as they pulled him and he groaned in pain. He couldn't help it, but he knew it meant trouble.

'Hey, he's awake.'

'Throw me the rag then.'

Ethan saw a fistful of cloth coming towards his face and was then hit by the acrid stink of chemicals as it was pushed over his nose and mouth. He tried to squirm away from it, but it was no good, and all his protesting was muffled by the rag. He tried to hold his breath as the fumes made his eyes water, but it was useless. Soon everything swam again and he saw the ground approaching far too fast.

'My wrist is fine,' said Johnny. 'Get me back on the streets now, Sam.'

Sam shook his head. 'I've lost Ethan. I'm not about to risk losing you too.'

Having picked Johnny up, Sam had raced the team back to the hangar, then called Gabe. He was on his way and had given strict instructions for them to do nothing until he arrived. But that hadn't stopped the team trying to work out what their next steps should be.

'Johnny's our best chance,' said Kat. 'Luke's too old and they're not interested in girls, so Natalya and me can't do it either. We haven't got a choice, Sam.'

'Kat is right,' said Natalya. 'If we are to find Ethan, then we must send Johnny and hope that he also gets taken. It is the logical thing to do.'

151

But Sam stood his ground. 'We've put out details of the van, so we should hear something soon. No one does anything until Gabe arrives.'

'Of course they could've switched number plates,' said Luke. 'If this is as organized as we think it is, then I would put money on them doing that while in the woods with Ethan.'

Johnny came in again. 'It's just a sprain,' he said. 'All it needs is some good bandaging and I'll be fine. I know the streets now. I can blend in. I'm our only option, Sam.'

'And waiting for Gabe is just wasting time,' added Kat. 'Ethan's out there alone. No backup. Nothing. We need to get moving!'

The sound of car tyres on gravel cut through the conversation.

'Here comes the cavalry,' said Johnny, unable to disguise his sarcasm. 'And I can't wait to hear his crap excuse about why Eth's tracker was fitted so badly it came out.'

Without a word, Sam left the team and went to let Gabe into the house.

Once more, Ethan woke to darkness. His face felt bruised and he remembered seeing the ground coming up to hit him hard as he'd blacked out. Whatever had been on that rag had been enough to send him to sleep real quick. He wasn't blindfolded, not that it mattered; wherever he was, the place was pitch-black. He couldn't see a thing.

He shivered and realized that he was soaking wet with water. His nostrils stung with the reek of fuel in the air. And he could taste salt in his mouth. The hum of an engine was everywhere.

I'm near the sea, he thought, at the same time as the

movement of what he was lying on made him realize he was no longer in the van. He was lying in the hull of a boat and it was moving. He wasn't *near* the sea at all; he was bloody well *on* it.

With that thought, Ethan felt what hope he had of getting out of this, of the team finding him, snuff out like a candle. Not only was he without a tracker for the rest of the team to trace him, but he was also now about to be floated off to God knows where, probably some foreign place with a dodgy government owned by the criminal underworld. Just how the hell was he going to get out of this? His chances seemed to be decreasing with each passing moment. This wasn't exactly how things had been planned.

A moan in the darkness close by knocked Ethan from his thoughts. Wherever he was, he wasn't alone. But were they friendly, or just another heavy waiting for a chance to kick him half to death?

Ethan stayed calm, listened.

Something knocked against his leg and a voice called out, 'Who's that? Where are you taking me? Talk to me, you bastards!'

The voice was male, young and seriously pissed off. Ethan waited until it had calmed down a little before he spoke.

'Who are you?' he asked.

'Why the hell should I tell you? Who are *you*? Are you with those gorillas who threw me in the back of a van?'

'I'm Ethan. And I'm in the same shit as you.'

'How am I supposed to know you're telling the truth?'

'Because I'm tied up and lying in the bottom of this boat and I'm guessing you are too, right?'

The other voice went quiet, but when it came back, it still had an edge to it; this was someone who sounded like it was him versus the world. 'I'm Rick. So what's going on, Ethan? And where the hell are we?'

'I haven't a clue,' Ethan lied, working to keep with his cover story. 'All I know is that I got yanked off the street, roughed up and now I'm here, wherever *here* is. What happened to you?'

'Same story,' said Rick. 'I'd had a smoke to warm up, was trying to bed down for the night when they just grabbed me. I didn't have a chance. Not that it stopped me having a go. I think I managed to punch one of them in the face.'

'They hurt you?'

'No one can hurt me,' came Rick's reply, and Ethan could tell those words were spat into the dark, not just said. Whoever this Rick was, and wherever he'd come from, he had an attitude you could sense a mile off. He was a prickly bastard, that was for sure. Rick was quiet for a second, then said, 'I've survived on my own for two months on the streets, since I walked out on my parents, out of my home. It can't get much worse.'

Ethan briefly wondered what must have been going through the minds of Rick's parents, how they'd coped these past two months without a word from their son. From the little he'd heard, the only thing keeping Rick on the street was misplaced pride. He thought how his mum would've reacted if he'd gone missing for so long. That small thought fired up his determination to find a way out of this and get home. And not in a body bag, either.

'Where are they taking us?' asked Rick.

'I was going to ask you that,' said Ethan as the motion of the boat started to make him feel sick, his head spin. It felt like it was riding a serious swell, and with every rise and fall Ethan could feel himself getting closer and closer to throwing up. Though he wasn't sure if it was the boat's fault, or the thought of just how serious the situation he was in now really was.

The warm, sharp scent of fuel, mixed with the sea and the rocking of the boat, meant Ethan had a real fight to hold on; being physically sick would drain the energy from him and he wanted to lose none of the little he still had left. But it was no good; nausea washed through him, his head span, and he emptied his stomach. The reek then got a whole lot worse.

Sweating now, Ethan tried to focus his mind on something other than chucking up again. 'You notice anything about the people who grabbed you?' he asked. 'What about the van? Were you conscious when they put you in here?'

'All I know is what I've already told you,' Rick replied.

The cry of seagulls cut into the moment and Ethan then heard, far off and very faint and low, the distant sound of a foghorn. It made the whole experience even more eerie.

'What's that?' Ethan asked.

'Just seagulls,' said Rick.

'No, that horn,' Ethan replied. 'Far off.'

'Can't hear anything,' said Rick. 'What difference does it make?'

Rick sounded like someone who was permanently pissed off, but Ethan could do nothing about that. He had to stay alert to any clue that might help, were he to get out. Any clue at all. And if the sound of a foghorn was just that, then he was going to take note and remember it.

Some time later, the blare of the distant horn no louder, Ethan was able to make out the sound of the sea crashing and breaking against rocks or a cliff. Then the thrum of the engine changed, pitching high then low, high then low, like it was coming out of the water on the top of the swell. Then it changed again, sounding like it was echoing inside a cave, and died to a faint murmur.

The side of the boat knocked against something and Ethan guessed the journey had come to an end.

A hatch opened above and Ethan was blinded by the stab of torch lights.

Ethan saw a shadow approaching from the open hatch. Then strong hands gripped him and pulled him up and out with frightening ease.

And if he can do this, Ethan thought as he felt himself lifted up like a child, *then I'm going to make sure I do exactly as he says.*

18

'Stand over there!'

Ethan blinked as bright lights blinded him momentarily. Vision blurred, he did his best to comply with the command. He obviously didn't comply quick enough as a shove in his back pushed him up against a wall of rock.

When his eyes were eventually able to focus, Ethan could not only see Rick for the first time, but also where they'd been brought. Rick was tall and slim, with pale skin and long black hair. He was wearing a tatty army jacket that hung almost to his knees, black jeans, black T-shirt, black boots. Ethan had seen Rick's type before, hanging around school like their only aim in life was to suck in the light. He was either a goth or someone who probably spent most of his

157

time watching vampire movies. Ethan had a feeling they weren't exactly going to get on.

As for where they now were, they were standing outside a cave on a rocky outcrop lapped by black water. He could make out its entrance across a rippling pool, in which sat the boat he assumed had brought himself and Rick here. It was moored up against a tatty wooden jetty. The water looked deep and cold.

Catching Rick's eye, Ethan nodded. All he got back was the hint of a sneer.

Things, Ethan realized, were rapidly going from bad to worse to full-on shit storm. He guessed that even if the team had been able to trace the tracking device to where he'd lost it in the woodland, from that point on he was completely alone, nothing more than a ghost. The team would have no idea they needed to look out to sea. Or, for that matter, for a cave accessible by boat.

The man who'd lifted Ethan and Rick out of the boat came over and pointed along the rocky outcrop. Ethan was able to make out a tunnel just ahead. He didn't wait to be told and just turned and walked towards it, but Rick didn't move. Despite the size of the bloke with them, Rick, it seemed, still wasn't going to do anything unless under duress. Ethan heard Rick ask for a cigarette. The next thing he heard was the sound of the man slapping Rick across the face hard enough to make him stumble.

'What the f—'

'Move!' shouted the man and shoved Rick hard to make him walk alongside Ethan.

'Do yourself a favour,' said Ethan, 'and shut up, right? You trying to get us killed?'

Slouched deep inside his jacket, Rick said nothing, just scuffed his feet along the ground.

Along the tunnel, they were stopped at a door in the rock. After it was unlocked, the ties holding their hands behind their backs were cut and they were both shoved in hard. A moment before the door was slammed shut, a carrier bag was tossed in after them. The click of the lock sounded horribly terminal.

Ethan looked over to see Rick huddle down against the wall.

'Rick?'

Rick said nothing, didn't move. Just sat there, head down, face hidden behind a curtain of lank hair.

Ethan went over to check what was in the bag. What he found was the first good thing to happen in hours: food. And plenty of it.

'You hungry, Rick?' Ethan held out a sandwich, like he was trying to coax a wild animal to come close. 'There's loads here,' he said. 'More than enough for both of us. You want the pork pie or the steak and kidney?'

Rick, at last, pushed himself away from the wall and edged over. 'How do you know it's not poisoned?'

Ethan opened a bottle of water and took a deep swig. 'Because I'm guessing that they wouldn't go to all this effort to just poison us now, would they?' He handed Rick a bar of chocolate and a packet of crisps. 'They want us alive, though for what, neither of us know.' Ethan was impressed; he was getting the hang of lying.

Rick held what Ethan had given him like he was half expecting it to bite his hand off.

'It's good,' said Ethan, demonstrating by shoving a broken portion of the steak and kidney pie into his mouth. 'Eat it. It's not like you've been eating well anyway, is it? Beats scavenging and begging for food.'

Rick, still hesitant, took a small bite, but once he'd started, went at the food like he'd not eaten for weeks. Which, thought Ethan, he probably hadn't. But he still had attitude. Every time he spoke it felt like he was spoiling for a fight. Ethan could see why he'd been chosen. Feed him up, train him, and Rick would give anyone hell, regardless of their size.

Ethan sat back and let Rick get on with feeding himself. It gave him a chance to recover a little too, and the feeling of food in his belly gave his morale a much-needed boost. After the initial sense that everything was at last going to plan, to have everything go so drastically wrong was a killer punch to the gut. Ethan needed his strength to keep a hold on where he was and what he was doing. All he could now depend on was himself and the skills he'd learned from Sam, the team and Reg and Mal.

At last, Rick managed to stop himself from eating long enough to start speaking.

'So how the hell do we get out of here, Ethan?' he asked, pushing himself up onto his feet and walking over to the door. He upended a packet of crisps into his mouth and the crumbs spilled down the side of his face. The empty packet was tossed on the floor.

Before Ethan could answer, Rick lashed out at the door with the sole of his right foot.

'Let us out! You hear me? Let us out!'

He kicked again. The door didn't shift. No one came.

'Not like that,' said Ethan.

'Well, sitting on our arses isn't going to get us anywhere, is it?' Rick snapped back. 'If we don't get out now, who knows where we might end up?' He kicked again at the door, then yelled out in frustration.

Ethan was about to tell the idiot to sit down and shut up when the sound of the door lock being opened clamped his jaws together.

He turned away from Rick to watch the door swing open. He just about had time to see a man dressed in a long chocolate-brown coat and a wide-brimmed hat standing in the open space before Rick bolted towards the door.

By the time he got to the open doorway, it had been filled by two more men the size of tanks. They were both armed, Ethan saw, but their weapons weren't drawn. They caught Rick and kicked him screaming and yelling back into the cell to roll on the floor. He made to get up and have another go, but a heavy boot pushed him to the ground like a cockroach on its back.

Ethan turned to the door again and started to yell and shout himself, make it look like he was just as panicked as Rick. Then the man he'd seen in the coat and hat slid in. He was carrying a black cane topped with a silver ball. Ethan kept his thoughts to himself on the man's choice of outfit: he looked like a B-movie criminal, the cane making him all the more idiotic. Then something struck him, a flashback to what Sam had said about Mr X carrying a cane. Ethan knew then that he was staring up at the man on Gabe's hit list. He'd struck gold. All he had to do now was work out a way to get

161

out and back to the team before he too ended up washed up on a beach like that lad in the photograph.

'I see that you were hungry.'

Ethan said nothing, just nodded. It was grey-man time and he knew trying to escape now, putting up any resistance at all, would lead to nothing other than a boot in the stomach from the two guards, one of whom still had Rick pinned to the floor.

The man glanced at the other guard who turned out of the room and came back with a folding chair. The man sat down.

'This is good. You will need your strength. And I can see that you both have plenty.'

Mr X gave his hat to one of the men, placed his cane in front of him, then rested forward on it. Ethan was able to see him up close now that he was no longer hidden in the shadow of the hat's brim. He had deep, sunken eyes, bordered by lines and wrinkles. Yet the way he carried himself – with such an air of confidence and physical strength – made him seem considerably younger. Ethan concentrated hard; if he got out of this, he wanted that face as clear as a photograph in his mind; his description of Mr X would be invaluable to Gabe.

The man grinned and Ethan felt like he was staring into the face of a giant cat about to claim him for its supper. 'I wonder if either of you have ever thought what a marvel and spectacle the Roman games must have been?'

Ethan was caught by the oddity of the question, couldn't think of anything to say.

'Imagine,' the man said, 'the true thrill of mortal combat! Not this sanitized version we see before us now in boxing and wrestling, but a fight to the death! Where sweat made the ground slippery, and blood flowed!'

Well, thought Ethan, *at least I now know this bloke's clearly insane . . .*

Rick, despite still being pinned down, started to yell out. 'What the hell do you want with us? Why are you talking about gladiators? Are you mental? Let me go!'

Ethan kept quiet, but noticed that the man, this Mr X, was now staring at Rick, his eyes cold and black like balls of coal. Then, without a word, he stood up and walked over, his cane tap-tap-tapping as he went. The guard with his foot on Rick eased off and backed away. Ethan saw Rick's eyes flash to the open door of the cell. Then he saw Mr X raise his cane and point it at Rick, who hesitated and glanced at the other two guards . . .

Ethan held his breath, sure as hell that Rick was about to make another pointless break for it, when suddenly Mr X thrust his cane into Rick's ribs.

Rick screamed. And it wasn't just his scream Ethan heard, but a bolt of electricity that had raced from the man's cane to slam into Rick. And he held it there for just a little too long, sending Rick's body into spasms against the rock, causing him to graze his hands and bang his face hard, drawing blood. When the man eventually drew his cane away, Ethan was relieved, but it was short-lived; the man went in with his cane twice more. And after the third time Rick's screams were nothing but whimpers, and he lay weeping on the floor.

Ethan saw the cane then turn to point at him. He scrambled backwards to get away, soon found himself with nowhere else to go.

The man asked, 'Am I going to have the same problems with you?'

Ethan shook his head quickly. He was no longer acting. He'd seen what that cane was capable of and didn't want it coming anywhere near him.

'Are you sure?'

The cane came closer still. Ethan braced himself for what he'd seen happen to Rick, felt panic tear through him, closed his eyes, sweat beading on his forehead.

'Look at me.'

Ethan opened his eyes and saw the cane only inches away from his face.

'If you want to live,' said Mr X, his voice smooth and awful, 'then you will have to fight. It is as simple as that. It should be your single motivation.'

Rick's whimpering was the only interruption.

'If you do not want to live, that is your choice. Death, as I am sure you are both now more than aware, is very easy for someone like me to arrange.'

He turned and left. Then, without warning, the two heavies grabbed Rick and Ethan, whipping their arms behind their backs to be tied once more, only this time with rope. As Ethan felt it pull round his wrists, he quickly tensed his muscles. He was looking for any edge now, no matter how slim. And when the ropes had finished being tied, he relaxed and felt them give a little. It wasn't much, but he hoped it might be enough for him to play with and get free.

Then they were out of the room and being dragged further along the tunnel.

19

The tunnel twisted and turned and Ethan felt like he was being pushed through the stomach of a giant snake. The two men shoving him and Rick along didn't let up the pace, punching and kicking them at every opportunity. A couple of times Rick tripped and ended up on his knees. He wasn't there for long as rough hands lifted him like a bedraggled rat and dumped him back on his feet.

Ethan was doing all he could to memorize everything around him in the hope that it would be useful later on. He was also wriggling his hands and could feel them slipping free. But with every step he was getting more and more frustrated. Scared too, if he thought about what was happening too much, so he tried not to, and focused as best he could on doing the job he'd been sent to do. Even if it had turned into a total balls-up.

So far, all he had was: sea water, boats, the sound of seagulls, a distant foghorn and a description of the man with the cane that doubled as an electric cattle prod. He couldn't see how any of that would ever be useful. He no longer even had a clue about how long ago it was that he'd been snatched.

The tunnel started to rise, the slope jagged and rock-strewn. A door appeared ahead, but before they got to it, Ethan and Rick were shoved into another cell. It was empty, except for a few grubby mats scattered on the floor. This time, no food was provided.

Ethan tried to lighten things up a little. 'Room service isn't great, is it? Think I'll put a complaint in to the manager.'

Rick didn't laugh. Instead, he just curled up in a corner and rested his head against the stone wall.

Ethan wondered how long the effects of Mr X's cane would last and walked over, dropping to a crouch. He was still wrestling with the ropes holding his wrists. He was close to being free.

'We need to do as he said,' he whispered to Rick. 'Keep our heads down, just do what we're told. Trying to escape will only piss them off. I don't want to end up dead, OK? And neither do you.'

Rick didn't respond.

Ethan felt his left hand slip. He twisted some more, could feel the rope grazing him, but that didn't matter. Getting his hands free would be a sign to himself that he was in control of at least something. He wasn't sure if it was what Sam would advise; it was hardly being the grey man. But he needed to get his arms working again; it would stop him feeling so trapped.

The left hand gave a little more, then it was free. Ethan pulled his hands round to his front and slipped the rope off completely. The grazes had drawn a little blood but he wasn't bothered. He placed a hand onto Rick's shoulder.

'You OK?'

Rick jarred himself away from Ethan. 'Leave me alone,' he said, then looked up. 'How did you do that? How did you get your hands free?'

'Saw this thing on TV ages ago about escapologists,' Ethan replied, explaining to Rick how he'd tensed his arms against the ropes as they were tied. 'Was a long shot, to be honest; worked, though.' He untied Rick. 'Better?'

Rick nodded, rubbing his wrists.

'If we can get out of these,' said Ethan, hooping the ropes, 'then we can get out of here, right? We just need to keep our heads.'

'But that was just a piece of rope,' said Rick. 'Hardly the same, is it?'

'Yes, it is,' said Ethan, remembering something Sam had said during their two weeks training. 'It doesn't matter how impossible this all seems. Just break it down into smaller pieces and you'll be able to deal with it. Survive. Just keep yourself alert. Look for weaknesses.'

'Well, thanks for the motivational chat,' said Rick, and Ethan noticed that edge to his voice returning.

Ethan knew he wasn't even convincing himself, never mind Rick; after all, he knew what lay beyond that door. He'd seen the photographic evidence, even watched the movie.

And that made him all the more determined to stay focused.

An icy draught was blowing through the cell. To stop himself from getting bored as well as cold, Ethan started to pace around it in circles just fast enough to get his blood flowing. With each circuit he thought about what the rest of the team would be doing now. Tracing him, he figured, would be impossible. The only real options left to them would be to: send either Johnny or Luke in undercover in the hope of them also getting snatched; ditch the op completely and abandon him in the process; or pray that Ethan would do everything he could either to make contact or escape.

The one thing Ethan knew for sure was that Sam didn't understand the concept of giving up. He'd put a lot of time and effort into getting the team and Ethan trained up to do the job. Pulling the plug wouldn't even be in his mind. Not yet, anyway. No, he'd be spending his time focusing on the rest of the team, getting them prepared for the final part of the op so that if and when Ethan made contact they could rock and roll in seconds.

Ethan changed direction, and after a few more circuits, had come to a decision. It didn't matter if the team were looking for him or not; he would have to work out a way to escape. Even if the others were looking for him, he knew there was no guarantee that he'd be able to live long enough for them to find him. The thought of it gave him a new sense of purpose. This whole op now depended entirely on his ability to collect enough intel for the team and to get back to them with it before it was too late. And by *too late*, he knew that meant his death in a sick modern version of the Roman arena.

Ethan heard footsteps and then the cell door was unlocked. Two men entered and walked over to them. They both immediately noticed that Ethan and Rick were hands-free, the ropes that had tied them lying on the floor.

'Thought you could escape, eh?'

Ethan shook his head. 'My hands came free. The knot wasn't tight enough.'

'Well, this one will be.'

The two men grabbed Rick and Ethan, and once again their hands were pulled behind them and tied. Ethan tried to tense as before, but the rope was pulled so tight it made no difference. Rick swore as the cords bit into his skin.

'Move it.'

Ethan walked behind one of the men to the door of the cell. When they were outside, the door he'd seen at the top of the tunnel was pulled open. A thick blast of icy air hammered into him, sending a ripple of goose bumps across his skin. He followed the man out into it, ducking slightly to make it easier to walk against the wind.

They were outside, but he had no idea where. He could make little out except that they were on a flat area of sand and rock, and behind them rose a cliff. The world was still dark, though a hint of morning was creeping into the sky, so he had some idea at least of what time it was. Unless he'd been out cold for a whole day, it had only been a few hours since he'd been taken.

Ethan heard a buzz in the air and recognized the sound of helicopter blades chopping their way through the sky. Then out of the dark a chopper appeared, settling to land just in front of them. Knowing he was going for a ride dashed any hopes he may have had of the team tracing him; they wouldn't have a chance. This op was quickly moving from desperate to impossible.

Ethan felt a shove in the back.

'In, both of you! And don't think about running anywhere; the tunnel to this beach is only accessible by air or sea. So unless you fancy a bloody long swim and hypothermia, do as you're told.'

Ethan ducked his head and walked over to the helicopter. The door opened and hands grabbed him from above and pulled him inside. Rick followed him in, the door was closed and the helicopter lifted. Ethan felt himself pushed onto the floor as they left the beach, and would have enjoyed the familiar sensation of being airborne again if it wasn't for the knowledge that every turn of the rotor blades made it harder for the team to find him. An air trip could take them anywhere, and that meant not just the UK. For all he knew, they were off to the continent, or to meet up with a ship out in the Channel. It didn't look or feel good.

Ethan felt his stomach cramp up as panic did its best to kick him hard. He was on his own. The team hadn't a clue where he was. What was he going to do? And just how on earth was he going to escape now?

The sound of Rick muttering to himself brought Ethan out of his thoughts. When he looked over, Rick was fast asleep, exhaustion having finally caught up with him. Whatever he'd been saying, he'd done so in his sleep.

Ethan turned away. It was dark. He was tired too. And there was nothing he could do to change what was happening to them. But like Rick, he could at least rest. In the back of the helicopter it was dark and sheltered and warm so Ethan allowed sleep to take him. He was knackered, anyway.

The sleep didn't last long.

Ethan felt the helicopter land and scraped his eyes open to see the door pulled wide and the early signs of daylight creep in. But that was all he saw before a bag was pulled over his head and he was booted out.

After the almost hypnotizing hum of the helicopter, it took a few moments for Ethan to adjust to what he could now hear. It was definitely the sea, and through the weave of the bag over his head he could make out daylight. So his eyes hadn't lied to him.

Someone grabbed him and walked him forward. He heard Rick behind him. They were pushed through a door, then down some steps. New noises now. Voices and grunting and the sound of clanking metal. It sounded like a gym, people exercising, using weights.

Finally, with one sharp shove, Ethan found himself stumbling forward into a small cell. It had a bed, a sink, a toilet, no window. But that was all the time he was given to acclimatize before a man walked in to join him.

He was dressed in black combat gear and carrying a huge whip.

20

The tail of the whip snapped at Ethan so fast he felt the pain half kill him before he even realized what was happening. It cut across his back, feeling like it was about to tear his spine in two. When it came again, Ethan tried to dodge it, but he was too slow. By the time the third strike thwacked him, he was in a ball on the floor and in complete agony, bright lights of pain scorching his nervous system to cinders.

'Name.'

Ethan wanted to scream, but the shock of the whip had snatched away his voice. The pain was singing in his ears. It was all he could think about, like every thought had been smashed to pieces by the whip.

The whip came again, and the pain was like being struck with a red-hot poker.

'Name.'

Ethan tried to say something, just to keep the whip from coming again. But all he could do was bubble a murmur of pain.

Another strike. Ethan felt it cut through what he was wearing, bite into his skin. He screamed out, couldn't stop himself, knew he was bleeding.

'Name.'

The pain was too much, but Ethan managed to force himself to speak his name. If he'd thought giving up that single piece of information was going to stop the beating, however, he was wrong. The whip just kept coming and coming and coming. Every time it hit home, it felt like he was being sliced in two. The pain burned through him like it was peeling his skin off in great bloody strips.

Ethan tried to block the pain out, kept telling himself not to give away anything that could be used against him, but there was nothing he could do to stop himself yelling out every time the whip struck home. The sound of his own screams echoed inside his head. He was already angry with himself for giving them his name. He couldn't give them any more. Wouldn't. All they'd ever get would be his cover, that was it. The risk was too high. Not just to the job, but to the others who'd been snatched. To Rick. To himself.

The man never muttered another word and eventually the beating stopped. Ethan was sweating with the agony of what had just happened. When he rolled over to find the man with the whip gone, the barred door to his cell slipping shut, pain tore through him again. Every movement made him feel like his back was broken and split beyond repair. He could feel it wet against the floor: blood. He half expected to see pieces of his skin scattered across the floor like bits of fresh meat.

A voice buzzed into the cell. Ethan recognized it immediately – the man with the cane and a sick obsession with Roman gladiators: Mr X.

'Hello, Ethan.'

The sound of his name being used by Mr X sent Ethan cold. The way he said it made it sound sickeningly as if they were on good terms.

The voice came again. 'That, Ethan, was your first lesson in understanding what will happen to you if you disobey us. We give no second chances. Your survival, your very life, depends on you doing as you're told. Do not test us. Ever.'

Ethan reached for the bed positioned against the wall and used it to pull himself up. But just those small movements made him cry out in pain. When he was eventually on his feet, he turned to where the voice was coming from. He was expecting to find a camera, but instead all he saw was a small speaker attached to the ceiling in a corner of the room.

'I leave you now in the care of my instructors,' said the voice of Mr X, and Ethan was sure he heard it smile. 'Good luck, Ethan. I will be watching you. We all will.'

No sooner had the voice finished than the door to his cell slid open again. Ethan turned to find himself in the cold presence of another man dressed in black combat gear. He had the sort of face that would only smile if you carved it on with a knife. And Ethan recognized it. He'd seen it in the photographs Sam had shown the team when he was back at the hangar. He was the one Sam had described to them as a general all-round nasty bastard: *Krav Maga* expert, ex-Israeli special forces, kicked out for gross misconduct.

The man came into the cell. Ethan stepped away, but the movement made him almost topple to his knees. His back felt like it was on fire and drops of blood were falling easily to the floor.

Ethan didn't even bother to try standing up. He slipped to the floor. This was no longer an act. He was in as much danger as any other lad they'd snatched from the street. The lesson with the whip had worked; he wasn't going to risk facing it again. And as for escaping, Ethan knew that if he was going to make any move at all, then he would be on one chance. And that would only be when he'd worked out a way to break away and get back to the team.

'Listen up, Ethan,' the man snarled. 'Your day works like this.'

Ethan just nodded; he wasn't going to argue. He remembered noticing scars on the man's face when he'd seen the photo, but up close the bloke looked like he spent his life picking fights with wolves. His skin was a mass of scars and although he wasn't huge, he looked solid, like he could survive a head-on collision with a truck.

'Day starts at six. You'll know it's time to get up because of the loud buzzer you'll hear doing its best to make your ears bleed.'

Ethan nodded again, said, 'OK.'

'Did I ask you to speak?'

Ethan shook his head.

'Didn't think so.' The man pointed at the cell door. 'This is automatic. It only opens if I say so. When it does, you go right, down the corridor and line up with the rest. Then just follow orders. Understand?'

Ethan nodded once more, but kept his mouth shut this time. The pain from his back wasn't going away and that made him start to think about what state he'd have to be in to try and escape at all. He'd have to do everything possible to keep himself out of harm's way, otherwise he wouldn't stand a chance.

The man commanded Ethan to turn round. Ethan obeyed and heard him approach. A hand touched his back and Ethan flinched.

'I can assure you it feels a lot worse than it looks,' said the man. 'You won't need stitches. The cuts and grazes will heal.' He walked towards the door and Ethan turned back round. 'It's five to six. When that buzzer goes, Ethan, you shift your arse, understand?'

The man didn't look for a response. But he paused on the other side of the door and glanced back.

'One more thing: as far as you and any of the other rat boys here are concerned, my name is *Chief*. Anyone else, you call them *Instructor*. It's that simple.'

Then he was gone, and the door slid shut.

Ethan was alone. The five minutes went by machine-gun fast and, when the buzzer sounded, his cell door opened and he did exactly as the man had ordered, charging down the corridor.

What he found at the end of it turned one shitty day into one disaster of a week.

* * *

'It's been a week, Sam,' said Kat, 'and we've still got nothing. What the hell are we going to do?'

She was sitting with Sam in the Defender, and about to be dropped off to replace Natalya, who was coming to the end of another four-hour stint of keeping an eye on Johnny.

'*This* is what we are going to do,' said Sam, 'and it's all we're going to do. We have no choice.'

'Has Gabe come up with nothing else? Nothing at all?'

Sam shook his head. 'No trace of the van was found. And the fact we don't like it doesn't matter; Ethan's survival is in his own hands now. All we can do is hope that Johnny gets picked up.'

'This whole job is a mess,' said Kat. 'We should've done more for Ethan. The tracking device should never have come loose.'

'No point thinking about what we can't change,' said Sam. 'We've sorted Johnny with a tracker under the skin, so if he does get taken, then no way will it be found.'

'Pity we didn't do that before, isn't it?'

Sam let out a long, calm breath.

'Here comes Natalya.' Kat opened her door and slipped out of the Defender.

'We're doing everything we can, Kat, you know that.'

'Yeah, I know,' she replied. 'Trouble is we don't know if it's enough, do we?'

Ethan tasted blood in his mouth. Wiping it away with his hand, he looked over to his opponent, who was standing only a couple of metres away. He'd counted twenty or so others in the place. None of them spoke to each other. Even Rick had learned to keep his mouth shut – with good reason. Another newbie had arrived a couple of days after him and Ethan. He'd tried to talk to another lad. Without warning, a guard had come at him hard with a baton, knocking his legs from under him. Then he'd rammed the baton into the boy's stomach. The baton – like Mr X's cane – had sent a charge of electricity through the boy's body. Ethan could still hear the screams.

Ethan now couldn't remember the last time he'd seen daylight and was sure his skin was already going pale without the sun. He quickly lost track of the number of days and nights he'd been there. His world ran like clockwork to the louder-than-hell buzzer that drilled into his brain to announce not just when to wake up, but when to eat, fight, wash and sleep. Even shit. And security was maintained by strength of force from the instructors and their electric batons. It was more than enough. Surveillance cameras weren't needed, not when those who might have considered trying to escape knew full well the consequences.

It was the same regime every day: wake up, eat, fitness, fight training, lunch, then sparring. After that, any injuries would be checked, dinner would be had, more fitness to really finish them off, shower, then bed. Meals were taken on metal trays and Ethan demolished each and every one, couldn't remember what any of it tasted like. He knew his body needed all the energy it could get; it was getting the living hell beaten out of it.

In addition to food, he was living on supplements, all designed to improve his performance: protein shakes, creatine, pro-hormones and various other powders mixed in water he had no idea about.

As for the instructors training them, they were monsters. The one referred to as 'Chief' oversaw the place with the efficiency of a well-run abattoir. Neither he, nor any of the others were afraid to show their faces and Ethan guessed the reason for that right away: they had no need to be afraid because, sooner or later, they believed all those trapped here who could identify them in the outside world would be dead. It was that simple, that horrific.

Ethan readied himself for another attack. Every sparring session was the same: paired up, each would be given a set time to attack the other, using what they'd learned that morning, and anything else they could remember or invent. Then they'd switch. And so it would continue, through dizziness, exhaustion and vomiting. It was a lot more bloody and violent than a practice drill down the local dojo. But that didn't mean injuries were left untended. The instructors were first-class first aiders, that much was clear to Ethan. And Chief had been right about his back; it had been mostly pain rather than actual injury, and had healed quickly. They were also taught to hold back from a killing blow; there was no point in bones being smashed and necks broken when they'd be doing that in the cage and bringing in the big money.

From the moment he'd arrived, Ethan had decided to work at keeping what Natalya had taught him to himself. He didn't want it to become common knowledge that he had a little bit of an idea about how to handle himself. Instead, he allowed his skills to slowly reveal themselves, as though he was learning them through the training they were getting from the instructors. So in the fight training, he'd stick to doing what he was told, although that wasn't exactly much: how to throw a punch, how to kick, not much else. It made the fighting dirty and uncontrolled, but so far Ethan had managed to keep himself pretty much unscathed. Chief obviously wasn't keen to impart his *Krav Maga* knowledge onto those getting into the ring; the fights wouldn't have lasted very long.

Now it was time for another practice bout. His opponent was huge; not an ounce of fat, muscles on top of his muscles. In normal circumstances, Ethan would've bolted, but this was anything but normal. And judging by the state of his opponent's face, and the scars and bruises that covered his body, he was a well-seasoned fighter. Ethan didn't want to guess at how long he'd been here. Or how many times he'd been into the ring and survived.

With a hefty right-hand hook, his opponent came in on the attack. But it was slow and sluggish, and Ethan knew that gave him an edge; if his opponent was getting tired, his movements and his ability to react would slow up.

Ethan dodged the flying fist easily, but he wasn't quick enough to turn his dodge and defence into an attack. He stumbled back, found his footing again, tried to clear his head.

Another punch; this time it was a left jab and was rapidly followed by a right knee. Ethan was ready. He side-stepped just enough to bring himself round to his opponent's right side. As the knee whipped past, Ethan came in with a sharp left-hand jab that caught his opponent in the neck. It wasn't textbook, but it was enough to knock him off balance. Ethan went in with another punch, but his opponent regained himself, dodged the punch, flipped Ethan round and grabbed his neck.

Within seconds, Ethan felt himself choking as the arm holding him squeezed tighter. And in that instant he was suddenly back in those moments after he'd been abducted, when he'd been taken out of the van to be 'softened up'. Then he'd held back, but he hadn't just gone through days and days of relentless fighting.

With a sharp twist Ethan looked up at his opponent and sent three sharp upper cuts with the heel of his left hand. The first only scraped past his opponent's chin, but the other two connected and bust the nose wide open. Ethan felt warm blood splatter down onto him. In the shock of the moment, as his opponent's eyes widened in agony, he grabbed hard onto the wrist of the arm round his neck, twisted his body and wrenched himself out of the hold. But he didn't let go of the wrist. Instead, when he was out, he twisted harder, brutally forcing his opponent to bend double with a yelp like a beaten dog. Blood was flowing freely from the guy's nose now, but Ethan wasn't about to stop. Couldn't. He went in with two hard kicks to the stomach, gave the arm one last wrench and sent him to the ground. He was about to go in again with another kick when powerful arms grabbed him, pulled him off. He struggled but it was useless.

'No point killing him now, Ethan,' whispered a voice close to his ear. 'Save it for the ring, eh?'

Ethan felt himself starting to shake as the adrenaline rush started to wear off. He looked down at the lad he'd just beaten. He was kneeling now, the front of his T-shirt a bloody mess, his arm hanging limp. Another instructor came over, picked him up, took him from the room. No one else batted an eyelid and the other practice bouts around the room continued.

The two instructors holding Ethan let go.

'We've never taught you that,' said one of them. 'We've kept you strictly to boxing, basic kicking skills. Our clients like the fights messy and unorganized and bloody. What you just did – what was that?'

Ethan shrugged, said, 'I don't know. Just reacted.'

But inside his mind was racing. What if they were suspicious? What the hell had he been thinking? But he hadn't been thinking, had he? He'd reacted, lost control.

'Bollocks,' said the other instructor. 'You knew what you were doing. Didn't look like karate though. More like Systema or *Krav Maga*.'

The other instructor said, 'Where's a kid like this going to learn Russian or Israeli self-defence?'

'He learned something somewhere though, didn't you, Ethan?'

Ethan was quiet. If this went beyond suspicion, he didn't want to think about what could happen to him or how quickly. But he couldn't think of a good enough story. So he just kept quiet and hoped.

'We'll be keeping an eye on you,' said the first instructor, leaning in close. 'We don't want any of that ninja crap in here, got it? This is real fighting, not Bruce Lee on wide screen.'

A buzzer brought the session to an end and Ethan felt relief flood him. He was bruised, disorientated and running out of options fast. He couldn't afford to be here for much longer. Not only was he getting close to blowing his cover, he knew he'd be put in for a real fight soon; it was only a matter of time.

That night, Ethan was grabbed and dragged from his cell, a bag thrust over his head. For a few moments, he thought he was about to get slotted, that he'd given himself away during the fight that afternoon and was about to be disposed of, sent to the fishes with two neat bullet holes in his head. But when his hood was finally pulled off, he knew things were – if that was at all possible – much, much worse.

21

The stink of bleach – trying but failing to get rid of the stench of sweat and blood – stung Ethan's nose like needles. He gagged, retched, managed to hold it in.

He was standing in the same place he'd seen in the film on Gabe's laptop. It was dark, but he could just make out the walls of the cage in front of him, the blinking red LEDs on the cameras surrounding it like the eyes of huge flies waiting to feast on dead meat.

In that instant, the mission died. All that mattered now was staying alive. And that was going to involve a lot more luck than Ethan dared guess at.

'It only gets worse from here, kid,' came a voice to his left. It was one of the instructors. He didn't seem to have a name. None of them did. Unless it was *bastard*.

A loud thump of a switch lit the dark with a flash of bright light. The cage was now visible. The room around it was a concrete-walled cavern with two doors, the one they'd obviously just entered through behind them, and one opposite, on the other side of the ring.

The horror of where he now was crunched into Ethan with the force of an A-bomb. His legs gave way, but he caught himself before he totalled on the floor. One of the instructors laughed.

'Got jelly legs, have you, kid?'

Ethan took a few long, deep breaths, managed to get a hold of himself. But he felt dizzy with nausea and panic. He couldn't change where he was, and that was bad. But what was worse, horrifically so, was that the only way he was going to get out of it was to beat whoever his opponent was. And from what he'd seen with the team, that meant . . . No, he couldn't think about it. Not yet.

A shove in his back caused Ethan to trip and after a few steps he was at the cage. A door in its side was opened.

'Strip.'

Ethan knew to question nothing and obeyed, pulling off what he'd collapsed into bed wearing a few hours earlier.

'Put these on.'

A rough hand threw a pair of red shorts at him. They took Ethan back once more to the film on Gabe's laptop. He forced himself to push back the memories of that fight as he slipped them on. Thinking about what had happened was going to be no help with what was going to happen very soon. And the only person who was going to get him through this was himself.

185

'Now get in there.'

Ethan didn't exactly have any choice as he felt himself manhandled into the cage and onto the damp floor. The door was locked behind him. No escape. Not until the fight was over.

Alone, Ethan paced the cage. It didn't just keep him warm, it gave him something simple, basic, to focus on. He was barefoot and the floor was cool. Then he did a few stretches, some warm-up exercises to get the blood flowing.

Voices made Ethan turn. In the bright lights shining down on the cage, he couldn't make out who had entered the room, but he knew it was his opponent. Then the cage door opened and they met.

Ethan recognized him immediately. It was the lad whose nose he'd smashed earlier that day. It was a bruised mess still, but the arm was fine and Ethan obviously hadn't damaged it as much as he'd intended; at the time, he'd wanted to tear it full out of the shoulder socket.

He looked seriously pissed off; his eyes were sunken and dark and made him look like a trapped animal ready to rip anything or anyone apart to escape. To Ethan, it was clear this wasn't going to be a situation he could negotiate; it was a fight for his life. Which, after all, was exactly what Mr X wanted.

For a few minutes, they both did some warm-ups, all the while keeping their eyes on each other. Ethan could feel his heart racing. It felt like it was trying to hammer out of his chest. If he was going to stand any chance at all against this gorilla, then he'd have to remember everything Natalya had taught him. He would be doing stuff that had never been covered in the scant fight training they'd all been provided with, but it was either that or get trampled. Sod the risk, his life was at stake! It didn't matter at that moment if Chief or the instructors became suspicious – he wasn't about to allow himself to get killed off. But the reality of what he'd have to do to win – and the thought of what might happen to him afterwards – threatened to short-circuit his brain. He had to ignore all of that. If he didn't go all out to win this, he'd be dead. Christ, he wanted to throw up . . .

A beep sounded and the voice that slipped eel-like into the moment was that of Mr X.

'My boys! This is the moment you have been waiting for; when you become not men, but gladiators!'

Ethan heard the buzzing and whirring of the cameras focusing in on him and his opponent as they faced each other in the cage. Whoever was watching was obviously now online. He couldn't imagine just how sick and evil those people on the other side of the cameras were. But he could easily imagine what he'd like to do to them if he found them.

The voice of Mr X interrupted his thoughts. 'The rules are simple: there are no rules. Anything goes. You are to win by any means necessary.'

Ethan stopped warming up, moved his hands to protect his face, got ready for the inevitable.

'If either of you are thought to be faking, or not putting in sufficient effort, your life is immediately forfeit.'

Ethan watched his opponent ready himself. He was no longer listening to the voice. He just wanted the fight on so it could be over. And quickly.

'The fight is judged to be over when one of you is out of

action. And by that, I mean, at the very least unconscious. Death would be preferable. Ready?'

Ethan narrowed his mind to everything Natalya had shown him: every move, every drill, every attack. Whatever his opponent threw at him, the little *Krav Maga* he knew was going to be his only chance. And he was going to use it.

A bell sounded.

Ethan was taken off guard as his opponent rushed him, ramming him into the cage walls, scraping his back against the wire, drawing blood immediately. Ethan felt like he was being pushed through a cheese grater. He brought his elbows down hard on the back of his opponent's neck. It did nothing. He felt himself being lifted up, the wire scraping harder and deeper into his back. Ethan tried again with his elbows, gave up. Pushing himself back against the cage, he was able to get his hands into his opponent's face, found his eyes and rammed his thumbs in hard. Then he brought his hand down hard on the already-damaged nose and blood flowed freely.

Ethan was dropped immediately as his opponent stumbled backwards, rubbing his face. He went to get up, but again his opponent was too fast; a foot caught him hard in the side, flipped him over. Then another foot came in, this one aimed at his exposed neck. Ethan rolled out of the way just in time, using the momentum to get back to his feet. He looked over to his opponent; that last foot aimed at his neck had been a killing move. It would have crushed his windpipe, maybe even snapped his neck.

They were both breathing heavily now. The fight had been going for only a couple of minutes, but Ethan knew full well just how exhausting a real fight was; every part of your body was being pushed to its limits, doing everything it could to survive.

When his opponent came at him again, he was more cautious and Ethan was able to regain his composure. They circled for a few moments, each throwing the occasional punch, deflecting them easily. Ethan went in with a combination left punch, right punch, knee, but nothing connected. His opponent retaliated, but was more lucky, and Ethan didn't get out of the way quick enough; the fist slammed into his nose and he felt it crunch. Next he tasted blood as the stuff ran down the back of his throat as well as down his face to the floor. For the first time he saw a flicker of a reaction on his opponent's face; it was a smile. Now they both had smashed noses. Snap.

The punch seemed to give his opponent renewed energy, and for the next few seconds, it was all Ethan could do to keep out of his way. But his luck failed and he slipped to the floor. He caught sight of the foot coming at him just in time to spin out of its way, using the momentum to bring his feet into the back of his opponent's knees, who dropped to the floor.

Ethan was up. It was the first decent move he'd managed since the fight had begun and he wanted to take advantage of it. He grabbed his opponent round the neck, squeezed, only to find himself flipped over his head to land on his back with such force the wind was thrown out of him like a burst balloon.

A heavy punch landed on his stomach, was quickly followed by another. They were done with such force that Ethan felt puke race up to his mouth. He was too slow to stop all of it and rolling to his side spat the acrid stuff across the cage floor.

Another attack came, but Ethan forced himself to his feet and got out of the way. The way this fight was going, he knew if he didn't get himself together – and soon – he'd be dead.

They were back to circling each other when something clattered into the ring at their feet. A chill ran through Ethan when he realized exactly what it was: two knives, each with a fixed blade about the length of his hand.

'To add a bit of colour to the proceedings,' came the voice again out of the darkness. 'But please be fair and take one each to begin with.'

Ethan's opponent was at the knives first, but in his rush to get them both, he managed to pick one up in his right hand and kick the other across the cage floor. Ethan raced to grab it, but it was knocked away.

Ethan watched his opponent start to prowl around him, keeping himself between Ethan and the knife still on the floor.

Staring at the weapon, Ethan willed his opponent to make a move. He wasn't about to attack himself, being unarmed. He had to wait and hopefully react in time to stop himself being skewered.

With a roar, almost as though he half expected his next move to be the one that won the fight, Ethan's opponent went in with the knife, aiming it directly at Ethan's stomach with a wide sweeping slash with his right arm. But Ethan got there first. Blocking the arm with his left forearm, he stepped forward and delivered two fast punches to the face, then sent two sharp kicks to the crotch. As his opponent doubled up and yelled out in pain, Ethan was still aware of the knife and knew then that this had to be the attack to end the fight. He couldn't risk it turning into a blood bath. So he went in again with another kick, dragging his opponent's face down onto his knee. His opponent recovered enough to come at him again with the knife, but the attack was slow and badly aimed. Ethan grabbed the wrist mid-flight, then with all the force he could muster, twisted it down, and stepped in, driving it towards his opponent's own body. He sent another flurry of punches to the face, heard the knife clatter to the floor. Then, to finish off, he grabbed his opponent's head and slammed his forehead at him.

Ethan stumbled backwards, shoving his opponent away. For a second, the lad stayed on his feet, then he simply dropped to the floor and onto his face like a felled tree.

The fight was over. Ethan heard the cage doors open, was only just about able to make out the silhouettes of men grabbing him, leading him out of the ring, other men grabbing his opponent to drag him out unconscious onto the concrete floor the cage was standing upon. His eyes focused and he saw the state of the cage floor; it was slick with blood. He tried to turn, to see if his opponent was OK, but he was twisted away by strong arms.

'Forget about him,' said one of the instructors holding him. 'Nothing you can do that you haven't already done. You minced him good. The boss will be pleased.'

'What . . .' muttered Ethan, his smashed lips barely allowing him to speak. 'What's going to happen to him?'

He heard the gunshot as he finished the question.

'Like I said,' came the voice again, 'forget about him.'

Ethan's world swam. He pushed at the instructor, yelled out such a scream that his lungs felt like they were going to burst. The instructor held him, Ethan still struggled, then a backhand slapped him hard across the face. It stunned him to silence, but did nothing to take away the horror of what he'd just been forced to do. And the face of his opponent seemed to burn itself into his mind, forcing Ethan to see him, to know that he was now gone for good.

For the second time in Ethan's life, it had been kill or be killed. There had been no choice. His opponent would've killed him, had been trying to from the moment the bell sounded. There was nothing else he could have done. Nothing!

Ethan yelled out again and another slap caught him hard. This time though, it didn't just sting, it crushed every ounce of strength he had left, and if the instructor hadn't caught him, he'd have dropped to the floor like a sack of shit.

Then all he could do was sob. And when he finally stopped, the horror still stalked him and no matter where he hid in his cell, the face of his opponent was still bright in his mind.

Unblinking. Unmoving.

Dead.

22

'Another few days and Ethan will have been missing for two weeks. And we're no closer to finding him.'

Gabe was stating the obvious. Everyone knew that. It didn't make it any easier to listen to.

'What about your other team?' asked Luke. He was sitting with the others in the hangar, not liking anything Gabe was saying. 'The ones who traced the signal for the fight you showed us. Haven't they found anything?'

Sam chipped in, 'No. Nothing.'

Johnny leaned forward. He'd been brought back in after doing a full week on the streets. The job was important, but so was his health. He'd checked out fine, as had his sprained wrist.

'Send me back in, Sam,' he said. 'If we're going to have any chance of getting to Ethan, then we have to put me out there again. They'll come for me soon, I'm sure of it.'

'Maybe they will,' said Gabe. 'But when? Could be tomorrow, could be next month. We can't keep this op going on indefinitely. Questions will be asked.'

Kat said, 'You sound like you're giving up.'

'Well, we're not,' said Sam. 'Johnny, get your shit together. You're going in.'

Ethan was still in shock, wondered if he'd ever be out of it. The violence of what he'd experienced seemed to ring in his ears. No matter what he did or thought about, it forced its way in like a truck through a house of straw. It had shown him something though: the mission was screwed, and of that he was absolutely sure. He had to get out fast. Risking another fight in the cage was suicide. He'd been lucky. His opponent hadn't been. Next time, the odds could just as easily be reversed.

Trouble was, the thought of escape was a whole lot easier than the act itself. Ethan had been wherever the hell he and the rest of the boys were being kept long enough to realize that the idea of someone trying to escape simply wasn't an issue for Mr X. And so confident was he, thought Ethan, that he didn't even bother with security cameras. He'd noticed that almost immediately; security was down to the instructors and locks on all the doors. That was it. But the boys were kept under extremely close watch. Hell, they weren't even allowed to speak to each other in the canteen. And he knew, because he'd tried. A couple of days ago, he'd managed to get close to Rick for the first time since arriving, sitting oppo-site him in the canteen. Rick had been head down and troughing the food. Ethan had tried to get his attention, but when nothing had worked and he'd said Rick's name, a shadow had cast itself over the table and he'd turned to see an instructor standing over them. The look in his eye had been enough to tell Ethan that talking was off limits.

It struck him as just a little bit odd. Considering just how illegal this all was, wouldn't Mr X want to keep tabs on all his fighters? The instructors were mean, the complex under lock and key, but surely there was still that risk someone would break out, right? Then a thought struck Ethan. He, like the rest of them, had no idea where on earth they actually were. Ethan himself had arrived by helicopter, which kind of suggested that wherever they were, it was pretty inaccessible. And if that was the case, he thought, for all he knew outside the walls lay hundreds of miles of desert or jungle or even sea. Much to his own horror, Ethan began to consider the fact that perhaps escaping from the prison would be the easy part. Whereas getting from it and back to civilization was probably not just horrendously dangerous, but impossible.

He could not let himself think like that, not if he was going to stand a chance of getting back to the team. People were getting to and from where he was. As he'd come in by helicopter, perhaps that was the only transport used. If he could get out and stow away, he'd maybe have a shot. It would be a slim one, but he fancied his chances better doing that than having to enter the ring even just one more time.

From the moment of his arrival, Ethan had been noticing things, not just to gather intel for the team, but in case he could, at the right moment, effect an escape. The importance of everything he'd logged in his mind had now grown tenfold; that moment was now.

Ethan knew that all the locks were accessed using cards the instructors carried with them. And he'd soon learned not only the shift patterns of Chief and the instructors, but the layout of the place. The structure was circular. The cells occupied by him and the other fighters were all on the same floor, lined up along a curved corridor. Each cell was locked by an individual barred door. At night, a single instructor was always prowling, though Ethan had noticed that after a couple of hours the sweeping of cells with a torch would stop. The instructor was still there, of that he was sure; they just lost interest in walking a torch beam up and down.

From this floor they headed through a single door at the end of the corridor to everything else.

Through the door, narrow, rusting spiral stairs led up to the next floor, which contained a small central canteen area. From here two further doors accessed the gym and the shower and toilet block. One other door was on this floor at the far end of the canteen and Ethan had never seen it unlocked. As the other two doors led to rooms which had no other exit, Ethan was sure this had to be the way out. It was also the way their food must have been brought in, because no actual kitchen formed a part of where they were kept. And no doubt it also led to any quarters occupied by the instructors, though he'd noticed that at different times of the week, different instructors were around. He figured this meant they were on some sort of rotation system and dossed down in bunk rooms when working.

As for the location of the cage where the actual fighting took place, Ethan didn't know exactly; he'd been dragged there hooded up. But it had to be through that door and somewhere else in the complex; there was nowhere else it could be. Much like the server Gabe was so desperate to locate. If it was here at all, then it was also through that door.

With his mind totally committed to getting himself out and back to his friends, Ethan now noticed a chink in the armour of the place that he could exploit. He'd managed to survive another day of training and fighting practice, and he was down in the shower block to get scrubbed clean before being locked back in his cell to sleep. He was just drying himself down, doing his best not to make his aches and pains worse, or knock the tops off any scabs and start bleeding again, when he realized something; it was the only place in the whole complex where you were actually completely alone, as the instructors never bothered to follow you in. And at night, it was the place furthest away from everything else; you could smash up a cubicle or two and no one would ever know who was responsible. This was the first glimmer of hope for Ethan; all he had to do now was get one of the instructors into the block and deal with them without risk of being watched or overheard, nick their door card, and then go for it.

Ethan knew he would only get one shot at this. If he was caught, if it went wrong at all, he was dead. It was as simple as that.

Later on and back in his cell, when the lights were turned

out, Ethan went over to the toilet in the wall of his cell. With no camera checking up on him, he knew there would be no one to see what he was about to do, and in less than a minute Ethan had managed to stuff down a load of toilet paper, not just from his own supply, but also from what he'd taken in secret from the shower block earlier. Standing up, fingers crossed, he pulled the flush. For a few breathless seconds, Ethan watched and waited. He pulled the flush again. The toilet overflowed. The first part of the plan had worked. Now for the next – and altogether more risky – bit.

Ethan, aware that whichever instructor was charged with the night watch had stopped doing sweeps of the cells but was still in calling distance, started to moan and stumble around his cell; he wanted it to be as convincing as he could make it that he was ill and in serious need of some assistance pronto. Ethan also hoped that he, like the rest of the boys being trained up, was too valuable an asset to be allowed to go down with a serious illness. This was an expensive operation; no way was anyone going to let it go to shit over a stomach ache.

Increasing the volume of his moaning, Ethan started to bang against the bars of his cell door. Then he started shouting.

'Help! I need some help here; feel like my stomach's about to burst. Please, someone . . .'

It wasn't long before he heard the night watch approaching. And they weren't exactly happy.

'Hey, kid, shut up with the moaning.'

'My stomach,' moaned Ethan. 'It's killing.'

'Have a shit, then,' said the voice at his cell door.

'Can't,' said Ethan, his breaths sharp as though in serious pain. 'Toilet's knackered. Isn't working. Needs fixing. Please, help me.'

For a moment, the voice was quiet, then it said, 'All right. Stand back.'

A torch beam burst through the cell door. It looked at Ethan, then at the toilet.

'See?' said Ethan, coughing and moaning weakly. 'It's overflowing. Can't use it.'

The torch beam flashed back again at Ethan, blinding him.

'You look fine to me.'

'Just let me go to the toilet,' Ethan replied. 'That's probably all this is. I need to go. Seriously.'

Then, just when Ethan was beginning to think his plan was already screwed, the cell door opened. The torch light found him again.

'In front of me,' said the voice. 'And move! I don't want to be hanging around here all night, got it? And you try anything I'll cripple you. Got it?'

'I get it,' said Ethan, and made his way along the corridor and down the spiral stairs into the shower block, wincing convincingly with every step.

Once inside, he gave it a few minutes before he put the next part of his plan into action. And this was the bit that really terrified him. If it went wrong, *seriously* wrong, he could end up not leaving the shower block alive. His only advantage was the element of surprise. But that was it. This was his only chance.

Ethan got himself onto the floor, half out of the toilet cubicle, half in, to make it look like he'd fallen and smashed his head on the door. Then, after a deep, deep breath, he let out the best agonized cry of pain and shock he could. And lay absolutely still.

Ethan heard the footsteps, but kept his eyes closed, didn't dare move. Not yet.

'Oi, kid, get up, you hear?'

Not yet . . . not yet . . .

'Seriously, kid, shift it!'

Ethan felt a boot prod him, but still he didn't react. Then he heard something being unclipped; the electric prod hanging from a belt.

And that was the signal he'd been waiting for.

23

Ethan grabbed the foot of the instructor and wrenched it hard to the left with a violent twist. It caught him off guard and sent him to the floor with a shout populated only by swear words. As he landed, he lost grip of the electric prod and Ethan watched it clatter across the floor.

Before the instructor could get back up, Ethan was on his feet and stamped down hard on his stomach, heading over to grab the electric prod. But if Ethan thought he was going to get away with this nice and clean and easy, he was very much mistaken.

The instructor rolled left and sprung to his feet with gazelle-like ease. He looked at Ethan and smiled, clenching and unclenching his fists, then balling them up ready to let fly.

'You're dead, you know that, don't you? You won't be leaving this room till I'm scraping your stupid face off the soles of my boots.'

Ethan wasn't listening. He had to close this as quickly and silently as possible; he knew there was only ever one instructor on night watch, but he had no idea if the others, who were probably asleep beyond that one door he'd not yet seen open, would be able to hear what was happening. Going up against an instructor one-on-one hadn't been a part of the plan, and if another one came to help his mate, Ethan knew he was dead for sure.

With terrifying speed, the instructor was on him, pushing him with a flurry of punches that sent him stumbling back into the cubicle and onto the toilet. The instructor followed in, grabbing Ethan's head and slamming it sideways into the thin, chipboard wall. Ethan would've yelled out, but the thump stunned him. Dazed, but forcing himself to stay alert, he brought his foot down onto the instructor's own. It did no good; he was barefoot, the instructor was in boots.

More punches came. Ethan deflected most, but one caught him in the side of the face, knocking him backwards. This was going even worse than he could have ever expected. He was getting trounced.

The instructor brought his foot up to grind Ethan into the toilet itself, but Ethan dodged and went in, driving punches at the instructor's crotch. The instructor yelled out, more from surprise, but it was enough to allow Ethan to get out. Now the roles were reversed and Ethan had the instructor trapped. He didn't give him a chance to recover, driving a foot into the back of his legs. He dropped to the floor. Ethan sent in more kicks at the instructor's torso. He wasn't aiming for anything in particular, he just wanted to make sure the instructor was seriously out of action. Then, while the guy sprawled on the floor in pain, Ethan dodged out of the cubicle only to come back holding the electric prod.

The instructor turned to see Ethan holding what should've been on his belt.

'You wouldn't dare.'

Ethan looked at the thing in his hand. He knew just how painful and horrific they could be. Then he glanced back down at the instructor.

'You know what,' he said. 'I think I would.'

Standing back, and out of breath, Ethan looked down at the instructor unconscious on the floor of the toilet. But he had no time to contemplate what he'd just done. Dropping to the body, he stripped it, ripped his own clothes into rags and a gag, to make sure the instructor stayed where he was, then changed into the instructor's outfit. He'd never actually given any thought as to whether the clothes would fit or not, so was relieved to find that they did, despite the pain his feet were now in thanks to the boots which, despite the size of the man they belonged to, felt at least two sizes too small. The disguise would be useless if someone came up close, but Ethan hoped it would give him an edge if he was seen at a distance.

Double-checking the instructor one last time, Ethan gave him one more blast with the electric prod, then stuffed him into the cubicle and tied him to the toilet with the rags. He didn't want him gaining consciousness and making a break for it. In the pocket of the instructor's trousers that Ethan was now himself wearing, he found what he was looking for – what this whole escape plan depended on: the key card for the doors.

He slipped from the shower block and out into the hallway. From now on, everything depended on a whole world of luck and guesswork. It wasn't great, but it was all he had. The first part of his plan, the only bit he'd had any control of, he'd managed to pull off, but only just. He could only hope now that the rest of it went just as smoothly, but the next stage was a complete unknown. Once through that third door that led from the canteen, he'd be in unknown territory. He pushed away all thoughts of what would happen if he was caught.

Ethan headed from the shower and toilet block, went through the canteen and walked over to the single door. From all the information he'd gathered, he had to assume it led to the way out – which he guessed was also the way he'd been brought here in the first place.

At the door, he pulled out the key card. He had no idea what was on the other side: if he was about to walk out to freedom; or find himself surrounded, and then dead. And no amount of waiting around was going to provide him with the answer. Letting out a long, slow breath to calm himself down, Ethan slipped in the card, saw the little red light in the mechanism turn green and turned the handle.

Through the door, he found himself in a short corridor which headed off in a curve to his left. He followed it round, and within a few metres came to a number of doors in the wall on his left. He knew he had to check what was behind them, not just for his own safety, but for when he brought the team back to find the server.

At each door he listened before swiping the key card. Behind the first, he found a small kitchen area. It was well-stocked, but contained nothing more suspicious than fridges filled with food and a large cupboard dedicated to sports performance supplements. The second door led to what looked like a staff room. A few sofas were scattered across the floor and a television was bolted to the wall. But there were no bunk beds. Maybe the instructors didn't live on site at all.

Ethan slipped back out into the hall. The further along he moved, the fresher the air became. Then, just as he was getting hopeful, another of the doors ahead started to open.

Without thinking what was on the other side, Ethan quickly turned to the next door along, whipped out his key card, slipped it through the locking mechanism and dived through. Wherever he was, it was dark, but the window on the door was clear and in the corridor outside Ethan saw the one person he really didn't want to run into at all: Chief. He'd been lucky with the instructor in the toilet cubicle. He had a sickening feeling that with Chief no amount of luck would be enough.

Ethan gave him long enough to pass before he made a move. First he had a quick look at the room he was now in. With the light slipping through the window in the door, he was able to make out exactly what it contained: weapons. It wasn't a large room, but wherever he looked he saw things designed with one use in mind only: killing people. Shelves were laden with ammo boxes. Racks on the walls were filled with M16s and AK-47s. And everything looked very, very new. A thought struck Ethan; these weren't weapons for the instructors, because they didn't actually need any. No, this looked more like a showroom than anything. Perhaps this was where Mr X brought customers to check out his merchandise? For a moment, Ethan wondered if he could collect any decent intel from the room, but binned the idea sharpish. What he'd seen was more than enough, and he knew that what he already had stored in his head would get the team back on track with the job to bust Mr X.

He checked the door again to make sure the way was clear, then slipped out. Against his better instincts to get shifting, he edged down to the next door, the one from which he'd seen Chief emerge, and pulled out his key card.

Ethan slipped into the room. It was quiet except for a faint electronic hum and clicking. He waited for his eyes to accustom themselves to the darkness, then shapes started to appear: computer screens, green and red LEDs blinking. Was this where Mr X kept the intel Gabe was so desperate to get his hands on? It had to be, he thought. Why else would a place like this have a room stuffed full with computers? He'd look forward to telling Gabe all about it. He also remembered that if he got the team here, then it would be Kat sorting this room out and downloading the intel Gabe was after.

The thought of turning this mission into a success gave Ethan renewed sense of purpose. He slipped out of the room, turned left and continued along the corridor. Two further doors lay ahead, one again to his left, the final one at the end of the corridor and directly in front of him.

Ethan opened the first door. Inside, the darkness was

thick, but that wasn't what bothered Ethan; it was the smell. His mind was instantly run through with memories of his fight in the cage, his opponent's face, the sounds and smells and terror. He didn't bother to look further, or even find a light switch; he knew exactly where he was – the room that contained the cage.

Ethan forced away the horrors of that moment and backed out of the room. He couldn't allow himself to get swamped by them, not now. Later perhaps, but right now, all that mattered was getting out.

Back in the hallway Ethan turned to the final door. On the other side he found himself faced with a sweep of stairs heading upwards. And there was a definite draught now; it was bitingly cold. Ethan climbed the stairs. At the top he found one final door. The key card opened it and he walked through.

A fresh wind swept into Ethan and he gasped. It tasted so different to the air he'd been breathing down below. He could see stars above and was almost overcome by the sense of vast openness.

Ethan steadied himself against the door and allowed his head to clear. The air was a shock, not just because it was so cold, but for tasting so damned good. He drank it into his lungs. It was filled with the smell of the sea and Ethan soon realized that the sea surrounded wherever he was. If the place was built on an island, just how the hell was he going to get off now? He knew they'd arrived in a helicopter, he'd known they were by the sea, but he hadn't for one minute thought he was on an island! How the hell was it possible for anything else to go so wrong?

Ethan was annoyed, angry and scared all at once. He remembered now Gabe saying there was a possibility that the facility was offshore, and he cursed himself for being so stupid. It became suddenly very clear why he had only found one instructor and the Chief at the facility that night; they didn't expect anyone to escape, because escape was actually impossible. So what was the point of staffing it?

Running round the outer edge of the structure, glancing down now and again to the crashing white tails of the waves far below, desperate to find something, a boat – anything – to help him escape, Ethan heard a sound humming in the dark. He recognized it immediately and, making sure he was as well hidden as he could be, started to scan the skies for an approaching helicopter. He watched it coming in and, in the last few moments of its final approach, saw a dimly lit helipad area light up with red landing lamps in the shape of an 'H'. Without that, thought Ethan, there was no way anyone would be able to find this place in the dark. And leaving the lights off till the last moments no doubt limited the possibility of the helipad being spotted by other aircraft.

When the helicopter was down, Ethan watched as it was unloaded: a lad with a bag over his head, shaking with cold and fear, was led by two instructors to the door he'd only minutes ago emerged from. But none of that was as important as the fact that, sitting only a few metres away from him, was his only way out.

The pilot had remained in the helicopter, but with the sound of the rotors as his cover, Ethan knew he had a chance of getting in without being noticed. It was a risk, but one he had no choice but to take.

Ethan dashed across from where he was and slipped silently into the rear of the helicopter, burrowing himself under some old tarpaulins for cover. He knew now that all he could depend on was luck. The new arrival would be taken to a cell, Ethan's absence would be noticed and the missing instructor would be found. Then all hell would break loose. Ethan had no more cards to play. All he could do was sit in the dark and hope.

And he wasn't a moment too soon as he heard someone climb up to sit next to the pilot. The engines thrummed into life and the helicopter lifted off.

Ethan lay as still as he could. He had no idea where he was now heading, but the fact that it was away from where he'd just escaped was good enough. From where he was lying, he could just see through the windows in the door of the helicopter and he watched as the blackness of the sea soon gave way to land, dotted with the lights of villages, streets, roads and towns. All he had to do now was stay hidden, wait for the thing to land, then get the hell out and fast.

Without warning, the helicopter bucked and shook, dropping in the sky, before continuing on its heading. But that little movement was all that had been needed for Ethan to be kicked out from his hiding place and lose the only protection he had – his electric prod. It skidded across the floor, but amazingly, neither pilot nor co-pilot noticed and Ethan shuffled as quietly as he could back under the tarpaulin. Then he spotted something strapped to the wall of the helicopter cabin within arm's reach: a parachute rig, probably for use in emergencies only. A thought struck him; why wait until the thing landed and risk getting caught and shot, when instead, if he could just get to that rig and strap it on without being noticed, then wait until the helicopter was flying over land, he could be out through the door and dropping to safety . . .?

24

With an eye on the pilot and co-pilot in the cabin, Ethan reached up for the rig. It wasn't exactly state-of-the-art, but it would do. For a moment he thought about the risk; he knew nothing of the rig, where it was from, who'd packed it. And so long as he made sure he was jumping over dry land, he'd be fine; land at sea and he'd be dead in minutes. But none of that mattered; this was his best chance yet to get the hell out and save his own life using the one skill he knew he could depend on – skydiving.

Ethan strapped on the rig. He didn't have Luke or Johnny here to check it for him, so he ran over what he'd done himself, double-checking everything in a way that would make even Luke proud. And the thought of the team, of what they'd say when he told them what he'd been through, brought a grim smile to his face. He'd survived, and he sure as hell was going to return with some payback.

Ethan looked at the door. He could see the handle; all it would take was a single yank and it would slip open, but he'd have to be quick. He knew that as soon as he made his move, the two blokes flying the helicopter would feel the shift of weight, hear the door and see him jump.

Slowly, ever so slowly, Ethan slipped across the floor until his hand was able to reach the door handle. Through the windows in the door he could see below him the lights of towns glinting and the headlights of cars zipping down roads. He could also see the coastline.

Ethan hadn't a clue how high he was and, with no altimeter, this jump was going to be half guesswork, the rest pure luck. And it was dark. Ethan had done night jumps, but never from a helicopter at an unknown altitude without a DZ in sight or an LED to make sure aircraft could see him in the air. This jump would be something he'd dine out on for years. More importantly, it might even make Johnny jealous.

If he survived it.

Ethan shot a final look at the helicopter cockpit, said a prayer to anything or anyone that was listening, then heaved the door open and pushed himself out into the cold, dark air . . .

The night sucked him out of the helicopter like it was hungry and Ethan immediately lost all awareness of where he was in the sky. But his training took over and he arched his back, got himself stable. The sound of the helicopter disappeared, swamped by the noise of the air rushing past him as he accelerated to terminal velocity.

Ethan looked up and was just able to catch sight of the lights of the helicopter. Below him, he could see the blackness of the sea beyond the coastline and the lights of a small town or village. It was the only guide he had to give him any sense as to how far away he was from slamming into the ground.

He adjusted his course, decided the best plan would be to hope that if he aimed just to the side of the village, he'd end up in a field rather than feet-first through someone's roof. He tried not to think about all the other things he could hit, like electricity pylons and telephone wires or rivers.

Reaching round to release the drogue that would rip the main canopy out of the rig when it grabbed air, shocking his body from 120 mph to 10 in only a few seconds, he stopped; if he pulled too early, there was a chance the pilot in the helicopter would spot him. They'd have seen him leave anyway when he'd ripped open the door; he didn't like the idea of them sweeping back round to try and ram him out of the sky. Or slice and dice him with the blades of the helicopter.

Ethan didn't want to draw any attention to himself, so he stayed on his current heading and waited until the very last second to deploy. It was a risk he knew could cost him his life, but it was a risk he had no choice but to take.

With one last glance up behind him, he pulled the ripcord. The main grabbed air, yanked him hard. He felt himself slowing down rapidly, then a few seconds later everything was dark. He couldn't see a thing!

Ethan knew he was in the dark zone, the air space below one hundred feet where ambient and moon light is lost. *Crap!* He was closer to bouncing than he'd realized, didn't want to think about the altitude at which he'd deployed his canopy. He desperately pulled at his steering lines to slow his descent, then the ground rushed up at him like it was trying to kick him back up to the helicopter and he hit the deck.

The world became a tumbling mess. Ethan's landing was chaotic and he rolled and tumbled forwards like a drunk circus entertainer. The wind grabbed at his canopy, dragged him sideways. Twisting round, he managed to dig his feet into the soft earth of the field he'd slammed into and kill the canopy completely. But he didn't have time to feel any sense of relief, or even rest a moment. He had to find out where he was and get back to the team.

Jumping up, he rolled up his canopy, threw it over his shoulder, then made his way across the field to the lights of the village. On the way he passed under some electricity pylons; he didn't want to think just how close he'd been to getting snagged in them.

Stepping out onto the road leading into the village, Ethan was relieved to find he was still in England and not, as he'd briefly wondered, in France.

Breaking into a jog, he made his way through the streets and soon found what he was looking for: a solitary phone box miraculously unvandalized. Pulling the handset free, he reversed charges to Johnny's mobile number. For the first time since he'd met him, Ethan made Johnny speechless.

'We found the tracker,' said Luke and flicked something to Ethan.

Ethan caught what was left of the tiny device. 'Last time I

saw this, I thought I was about to get a serious kicking. How time flies when you're having fun.'

He was sitting back in the hangar with the rest of the team. He'd been given no time to rest. Sam had picked him up, but had been about as talkative as usual; he'd voiced his approval of Ethan's escape, but given little else away. Gabe had wanted every detail Ethan could drag from his brain on what had happened to him, what he'd seen, and had jumped at Ethan's description of Mr X. When Ethan had described his fight in the cage, Sam's face had grown dark and serious.

Once over, Sam had suggested to Gabe that it was now time to send in the UKSF, but Gabe seemed disinclined to agree with him. He wanted the information on the server Ethan had found before anyone else got sent in. That was the priority and he wanted the team to continue with the mission and complete that part of it as well.

There had been no further discussion.

Ethan was then able to catch up with his Raiders team-mates, the best part so far being the hug he'd got from Kat. But even that hadn't been able to stop him thinking about the face of the boy he'd fought and the sound of the gunshot that followed the fight; both were indelibly burned into his brain.

Sam and Gabe now entered the hangar. Sam said, 'Ethan, I'm getting someone in to run a full medical check on you.'

Ethan didn't argue. After all he'd been through, and all the stuff he'd had to put into his body at every meal, he was happy to be checked over.

'Actually,' said Kat, 'you look in very good shape, considering.'

'Not really a surprise,' said Ethan, enjoying seeing Kat's

face again and the fact that his improved physique had caught her eye. 'All I've been doing is fitness training and living on protein shakes for the best part of a month. I'm knackered.'

'Well, I'm afraid we've got no time for rest,' said Sam. 'We need to move fast. I need you to fill the rest of the team in on what you've already told me and Gabe.'

Ethan leaned backwards against his chair, rubbed his eyes till he saw stars, then sat forwards again.

'OK,' he said. 'And Sam, I hope someone's taking notes, because after this, I'm getting my memory erased.'

25

'I have no doubt at all,' said Gabe, grave concern clear in his voice, 'that the man you described with the cane is Mr X. It could be no one else.'

Ethan said, 'It looked like he'd chosen his outfit after watching too many movies with over-dressed gangsters as the bad guys. If I hadn't been so bloody scared, I'd have laughed.'

'Your description matches him exactly,' said Gabe. 'Not just in the way he dresses, but his motives, his personality. And he's not just wanted for arms dealing and this little cage-fighting racket he's running. He's connected to at least a dozen murders.'

'Always with the good news, aren't you?' said Johnny.

Sam pulled out a map of the south coast and looked at Ethan. 'This is the village we picked you up from,' he said, pointing to the map. 'Can you tell me again what you saw when you escaped the facility, from the helicopter?'

'It was like an island,' said Ethan, 'but made of concrete. Sounds nuts, I know. It was surrounded by the sea and was definitely a large construction, like it had actually been built out at sea – but not far from the coast. When I was on the helicopter it wasn't long before we were flying out over land. And that's about it.' Then he remembered something. 'Oh, and when I was heading out, I'm sure I heard a foghorn or something in the distance.'

'Such a thing surely does not exist,' said Natalya.

'Well, it does,' said Ethan, 'because I was on it.'

Gabe leaned in and dropped a finger to the map. 'What about that?'

'What is it?' asked Ethan.

'Napoleonic sea fort. Built to protect the coast against a French invasion. A whole garrison could be housed in one. Not many of them were built. I think one was turned into a hotel a few years ago.' He pulled a laptop computer from his briefcase and booted up a search on the internet. A picture of a fortress surrounded by the sea flashed up.

'That's a shitting awful DZ,' said Johnny. 'We could go in with RIBs.'

'No, we couldn't,' said Sam. 'You're not trained in using them, we'd have the whole issue of having to scale the walls, and boats approaching fast would spook them much quicker than you lot dropping in from the sky.'

'But that's a seriously restricted DZ, Sam,' said Johnny.

'We miss, we're in the sea. And I'm guessing we won't have a sub waiting to pick us up this time, right?'

Ethan and the rest of the team looked over to Sam. He was quiet for a minute then spoke. 'Gabe, we need a satellite run on this place now. If it checks out, if we see any hint of activity, like this helicopter Ethan jumped from, then we're good to go. Agreed?'

Gabe nodded. 'The team's still the best option for this part of the op. UKSF will be called in afterwards for the cleanup. But for this bit, it's what you've all been trained for.'

'Good,' said Sam. 'Now, Ethan, what about when we get inside? What can we expect? We need specifics, OK? Number of x-rays and abductees, weapons, layout of the place. Reckon you can draw us a detailed map of the place and write it all down? The main thing is obviously the location of the server.'

'Totally,' said Ethan. 'It's not a big place. The layout is dead simple. From the roof, we go to the first floor which has the server, the room for the cage fighting, armoury, kitchen and staff room for the instructors. The rest is where I spent most of my time. Nothing much – just a small canteen, shower and toilet block, and gym. Then on the floor below that are the cells.' Ethan grabbed a piece of paper and a pen from Sam's desk and started drawing a plan of the building.

'What about security?' asked Luke.

'I don't think it's seen as a problem,' explained Ethan, 'probably because of the fact that the place is out at sea; so escaping is pretty much impossible.' He then flashed a look at Kat. 'But not totally impossible, as you can see. The place has no surveillance, and at night only one instructor is on guard, along with the Chief, who runs the place. Though I'd guess he isn't there every night.'

Gabe said, 'You'd better be prepared for additional security when you go back in. Your somewhat elaborate escape, Ethan, will have spooked them. They won't be keen on allowing such a thing to happen again. Expect more resistance, probably armed.'

'Good point.'

Johnny laughed and said, 'You know, after what you pulled off, Eth, I reckon we're going to have to keep an eye on you.'

'Why's that?'

'If we're not careful, you'll go all *Mission Impossible* on us.'

'This is no laughing matter,' snapped Gabe suddenly, breaking with his usual calm demeanor. 'In many ways your actions, Ethan, could well have blown our cover completely. We're going to have to work damned hard to recover this operation at all.'

Was Gabe saying he'd have been better to stay put? 'You make it sound like I shouldn't have escaped!' Ethan said.

'There's escaping, Ethan, and there's making a whole song and dance about it.'

'*What?* Have you got *any* idea what I went through in there? I—'

Sam stepped in. 'Ethan . . .'

But Ethan wasn't having any of it. 'No, Sam! I'm the only one here who knows exactly what I've just been through. I was abducted. I was beasted every day, with the threat of being whipped or electrocuted hanging over me. I was beaten up within an inch of my life and it was me who had to climb into that cage and come out alive no matter what!

And despite all that, I managed to get the hell out and bring back the intel you and Gabe sent me to get in the first place! I had to kill someone! So, Gabe, here – none of you – have a clue!'

'That's not what I was implying,' said Gabe, his voice calm again. 'We know you have been through a terrible ordeal, Ethan. My apologies.'

'Terrible ordeal? Are you mental?'

Gabe sighed. 'I'm simply saying, Ethan, that although I understand *why* you had to escape, and indeed applaud that you were able to effect it at all, I just wish it had been a little less noisy. Beating up and binding that instructor, then skydiving out of a helicopter in the middle of the night, can hardly be classed as covert.'

'I had no idea where I was,' said Ethan, already tiring of explaining his actions. 'I was bloody lucky the helicopter arrived at all, otherwise I doubt I'd have made it any further. And I think we can all guess what would've happened to me had I been caught, right? You saw the video, and I can tell you it really was kill or be killed in there.'

Gabe said nothing else, just folded his arms, sat back in his chair.

'Luckily,' said Sam, 'the cover story is already sorted. We've put out a report on the news about someone matching your description, Ethan, being found washed up dead on a beach. We also mentioned the fact he was found with the remains of a skydiving rig still attached, and hopefully that will do the job.'

Ethan said, 'That's believable, I guess. When I jumped, if I hadn't known what I was doing, I could just have easily ended up in the sea; the village I landed by was right at the coast.'

'Exactly,' said Sam. 'It's the best we can do, so we'll leave it at that. Anything else?'

Ethan thought for a moment, then turned to Natalya. 'Your training saved my life. I've no doubt about that at all.'

'I am glad to have been able to help,' Natalya replied. 'We will continue with your training once this is over, yes?'

'I've been thinking about that,' said Sam. 'When we draw this to a close, I want you, Natalya, to sort out regular CQC training for the rest of the team. You happy with that?'

'Of course,' said Natalya.

Sam turned to Gabe. 'Let's get the check on that fort now.'

Gabe nodded. 'There's nothing else close enough anyway that matches what Ethan described. I'll sort the satellite now.'

An hour later, Sam brought the team together. 'Well, against the odds, it seems we might just pull a bunch of roses out of what was beginning to smell like a huge sack of shit.'

A faint laugh echoed around the room from the team.

'We've got Ethan back,' continued Sam, 'his intel has confirmed everything we suspected, and he's given us first-hand knowledge of where we're going and what we'll be dealing with when we get there. If the satellite images check out, we should be on for tonight. This will be a drop to a restricted DZ. So I'm betting you can all guess what we're going to be doing for the rest of the day, right?'

Kat raised her hand.

'Ethan; about the computers. What am I actually going to be dealing with?'

Ethan looked over. 'From what I saw,' he said, 'the room was stacked with kit. Lots of impressive flashing LEDs and the sound of fans keeping everything cool. Sorry I can't be any more detailed; it's not exactly my area of expertise.'

'So I'm kind of on my own once we get there, then,' said Kat.

'I guess.'

'It's not a problem, it's a challenge,' said Johnny.

'It could be both,' said Kat. 'Gabe; what am I being sent in with?'

'Enough to get the information we need and cripple the whole system automatically,' Gabe replied. 'Hopefully it'll just plug and play.'

Luke looked up. 'Gabe, can you get me the rough measurements of the size of the surface of that sea fort? We can mark it out in the clearing behind the house. We've not got time to build a structure to land on, but it'll do.'

Gabe nodded.

'Just out of interest,' asked Kat, 'if we're jumping onto this thing at night, how are we supposed to find it in the dark?'

'Sorry,' said Ethan. 'I forgot that the helipad is lit. It's not bright, but it'll be enough for us to find it.' A thought crossed his mind. 'Sam, I know jumping from a heli will help us get on target from the off, but won't the noise of the rotor blades give us away?'

'We'll be at ten thousand feet,' said Sam. 'They're not about to think it's anything other than the coastguard or a private charter. And we'll only hover long enough for you lot to exit.'

The room fell quiet.

'Well,' said Sam, 'if there are no other questions . . .'

No one spoke.

'Good,' nodded Sam. 'Then let's get moving!'

Ethan bundled up his skydiving rig and walked over to Johnny. Once the briefing had finished, and the medic had given him the once-over and all-clear to stay in action, he'd managed to grab a couple of hours' shuteye. Then he'd been up and skydiving almost immediately. Amazingly, he didn't really feel tired, the excitement of what they were now doing energizing him better than any number of energy drinks laced with glucose and taurine.

'Piece of piss, hey, Eth?' said Johnny, his rig slung over his shoulder. It looked like he was carrying the world's largest – and very dead – squid. 'That's the fourth jump and none of us has landed outside the area Luke marked out. We're doing a star formation next as that's how we'll be going in; means we won't get too split up in the jump.'

'Won't be so easy at night though, will it?' said Ethan. 'I know the helipad is lit, but they're only very dim lights and we probably won't be able to see that until we're almost on top of the fort, and then we'll hit the dark zone and the bloody thing will disappear!'

'Nice to hear you're being so positive,' said Johnny. 'Anyway, it'll be visible once we're under the canopy, so long as there's enough ambient light around, and there should be because we're jumping close to the coast.'

'Town lights make that much difference?'

'They should.'

Gabe called from the house.

'Come on,' said Johnny, 'or he'll get all upset that we're not having enough fun at his party and send us home early.'

Back in the house, Gabe brought everyone together. 'I need to explain a few things before you go any further,' he said.

Ethan, like everyone else, listened up.

'This is a high-risk operation and it's one that few know about. I'd like to keep it that way for now. Your only job in going in is to get the intel. Only – and I do mean *only* – when we've pulled you out, will we call on the heavy guns to go in and rescue the abductees, and deal with the x-rays.'

'Why can't we do it at the same time?' asked Ethan. 'Surely it makes sense? I know my way around the facility. We could wrap the whole thing up in one go.'

'No,' replied Sam. 'Too risky. You'll stick to the job, which is to find the server and get the intel. Leave the rest for the boys who know best. OK?'

Ethan knew Sam had a point, even if he didn't really like it, and nodded agreement. He'd been in that place, knew what Rick and the others were facing. He didn't like to think that by leaving them there any longer than necessary they were placing them in any more risk. The thought that another two could be sent to the cage was enough to bubble up his anger. But he forced himself to stay calm. If they did their job well and quickly, he knew Sam and Gabe would send in the UKSF immediately, probably chasing in on the dust left by their own exit.

'It's the cleanest way, trust me,' said Sam. 'I know your skills better than you know yourselves. I don't want you going

225

all heroic and getting full of holes. Or getting any of those other teenagers shot. They don't deserve that.'

Sam let everyone think about his final point before speaking again.

'You're jumping onto the fort,' he explained, 'because as we've already discussed going in by sea is too risky. You've not been trained to use boats or done any diving – yet – so we're going to stick with what you know.'

Gabe said, 'You'll be jumping without LEDs as we don't want anyone spotting you coming in. I've cleared the airspace in that area so hopefully you won't be in any danger.'

Sam took up again. 'When you're all down Luke will deal with the entry door – I've sorted a fibre-optic viewing cable, so you can check all's safe on the other side, and we've got the electronic lock gun, so it should be a cinch. And you should now all be completely familiar with the layout of the place, thanks to the detailed plans Ethan drew up for us. Finding the server doesn't look like it will be a problem anyway, particularly as it's so close to the entrance. Kat will then do what she does best and download everything she can onto a high-capacity portable hard drive.'

'From then on,' said Gabe, 'all you need to do is buzz Sam on the chat-net and get back up top. He'll still be in the air, far enough away not to be noticed. He'll sweep in to extract you.'

'But the signal will probably be crap once you get inside that place,' said Sam, 'so you'll have to be outside to contact me. UKSF will be coming in on our coat-tails, so get in and get out quick. Don't get distracted. I want no heroics. And remember, avoid violent confrontation. Your strength lies in being sneaky as hell. If you meet an x-ray, gag and tag, simple as that.'

'Is there not a danger of us being spotted coming in to land?' asked Natalya.

'I don't think so,' said Ethan. 'From what I saw, they didn't have anyone on guard duty up there – there was nowhere up on top to shelter or anything.'

'We go in four hours,' said Sam. 'So let's get another couple of jumps in to make damned sure you lot don't screw this up from the off and just drown.'

26

Ethan was in the hangar with the rest of the team waiting for the good-to-go from Sam. Earlier he'd been desperate to get back to the fort and finish the job, but now he wasn't so sure. In many ways, he wanted to forget the place completely, erase it from his mind. He'd spent every moment there wondering just how long he had left to live, how soon it would be before he was sent to the cage again and his luck would run out. But he had to go back, had no choice anyway. His on-the-ground knowledge would be vital to the success of the mission. And this time, he was part of a team. It wasn't like he was being sent back in alone.

He forced himself to focus on the job and getting it done. He could deal with the repercussions of everything he'd experienced once it was over. And glancing round at the rest of the team gave him a confidence boost. They were all kitted up ready for the jump; black from top to bottom, including war paint and helmets with full-face visors, self-inflating lifejackets just in case, throat mics and torches to check their canopies once deployed. In addition, and because of Gabe's warning about the possibility of more x-rays being around after Ethan's daring escape, they were carrying plastic tags to deal with them, and flash-bang and smoke grenades, which were only to be used as a last measure. Outside, the night was drawing in.

A voice buzzed on everyone's throat mic. It was Sam on the chat-net.

'Right, listen up. It looks as if the weather's taking a turn for the worse, but we're going in anyway.'

Johnny squeezed his throat mic. 'What do you mean by "Turn for the worse"? Overcast with the risk of a shower or two, or the sky falling on our heads?'

'You'll be jumping in the rain,' said Sam, 'so shift it. We're going now.'

Everyone heard the sound of a helicopter starting up, and as Ethan ran out with the rest of the team into the darkening evening, he saw the blades beginning to turn, Sam at the controls.

Luke's voice came over the chat-net.

'Once we're aboard, everyone double-check their kit. And remember, when we exit, we'll be doing it in formation as a star, just like we practised earlier, with Johnny between Ethan and me, not circling like he would if we were at a competition. And watch your fall rate, everyone. Understood?'

The team pinched their throat mics twice, the double beep acknowledging they'd all heard what Luke had said and understood it.

'Good. When it's time to deploy, we'll star burst so everyone can find safe air. Then – and seeing as this really is the one thing we should all know how to do – it's just a case of landing safely without breaking a limb.'

'Or drowning,' said Kat.

The helicopter bucked a little as the rain came in heavier. It blew through where the team were sat and Ethan hunched himself against it. It was seriously cold.

'Ethan?'

It was Luke on the chat-net again.

'You're on point. We all know the layout, but you know this place. It's why you're here: getting us to the room with the server is your responsibility. Any x-rays, leave to Natalya and Johnny to deal with. Understand?'

'OK,' said Ethan. 'How long have we got before we get to the DZ?'

Sam's voice fizzed in. 'Five minutes! Ready yourselves. I want you in the air sharpish and the exit smooth.'

The team all slid to one side of the helicopter. Johnny and Luke stood outside on the helicopter's landing runner, holding onto the roof until the time came to jump.

A few moments later Sam called again: 'Thirty seconds!'

Ethan felt the helicopter slowing, his legs dangling over the side. He grabbed hold of Kat's arm – she was sitting on his left – and reached up for Johnny's arm on his right. Everyone else linked in. All that remained was for Luke and

Johnny to link when the time came to jump.

Then suddenly Sam called through with: 'Move it!'

A sharp nod from Luke as he grabbed hold of Johnny. Then the team tumbled into the black.

Picking up speed, the team soon stabilized, even though there were five of them linked together. Ethan felt the rain sting his hands like he was being attacked by wasps, but he ignored the pain; he'd had a lot worse than that over the past few weeks.

He looked at the rest of the team; in the thick darkness, all he could make out was five skydiving helmets, each one laced with streaks of rain. It felt as though they were floating; everything about them was pure, drenched blackness.

Ethan caught sight of lights far off; towns and villages beaming into the night in a definite line stretching left and right along the coast. The DZ was somewhere below them, a tiny black dot in an angry sea. He was looking for that faint red 'H' of the helipad, but he couldn't see it! Where the hell was it? So much for the ambient light, Johnny had mentioned; he could see jack shit!

A signal came from Luke. Ethan knew this meant that at the next ping from his audible altimeter the formation would split. Then he'd be on his own. He hoped to God he'd soon spot the DZ, otherwise he was in for a wet landing and crappy swim.

The ping came all too quickly.

The team exploded outwards, all shooting off in different directions to find safe air. Even though none of them were wearing LEDs, Ethan still double-checked the air above and around him before he deployed his canopy. The sound of it blasting open above his head wasn't as much a relief as was the sight that caught his eyes immediately beneath him once he'd slowed down to descent speed. It was the dimly lit helipad on the fortress, the DZ: a strange dark shape just sitting in the water waiting for them to arrive.

And Ethan was first.

As he came in to the DZ, he drove all thought from his head about it being in the middle of the sea, that on all sides was a high drop to waves that could crush him in seconds, and focused on his landing. He adjusted his steering lines, turned in, adjusted again . . . this was it . . .

Ethan heaved on his steering lines to kill his canopy at the last second and bring himself to a gentle touchdown on the DZ. If he'd been anywhere else he'd have yelled out in triumph, but he kept his mouth shut, deflated his canopy, rolled it all up. He pulled a silk stuff sack out of a pocket and stowed his rig and helmet inside it; that would make it easier to chuck onto the helicopter when Sam came to collect them. Then he got out of the way of the rest of the team coming in.

He headed over immediately to the door he remembered all too well; the last time he'd been here he'd been running for his life. It wasn't the kind of place he'd quickly forget. He also wanted to make sure that if anyone came through it, he was there to sort them out. And after the way the instructors had pushed him around, he wasn't going to hold back if they did.

Like huge black seagulls, Ethan watched the team come in to land in quick succession and soon they were all standing with him. Without a word spoken, Luke dropped to the bottom of door. Ethan watched him pull from a trouser pocket what looked like a length of thick, black wire and slip it under the door – the optical cable. A few moments later he removed it, stowed it and pulled out something that looked like a small drill – the lock gun. Luke placed this to the lock and Ethan heard the satisfying click of it giving in nice and easy. Luke then stood up and opened the door like the perfect host or butler.

'Over to you, Ethan; we're right behind you.'

Despite the serious nature of what they were now doing, hearing that from Luke made Ethan grin. The team were depending on him now, and he wasn't going to let them down.

It wasn't difficult to head straight to the computer room. The layout was simple and he'd been recalling it, drawing it and studying it since his escape. He hated knowing that lying just a couple of floors below them were the rest of the abductees, and he could do nothing to help them. But he knew Sam was right – they had to leave that job to the ones with the firepower. But it didn't make him feel any better.

Ethan led the team down the corridor, all of them silent as ghosts. At the door to the room with the server he nodded to Kat who slipped forward.

'Well, this was a lot easier than I was expecting,' whispered Johnny. 'Usually there's at least one bad guy to slug it out with.'

The team slipped in behind Kat as she crept into the room. So far they'd neither seen nor heard anything of any possible x-rays. Ethan was relieved; now that he was here, he wanted to get out as quickly as possible.

Kat was soon working at a keyboard and plugging in a small, rubber-covered black box.

Ethan asked, 'How long will this take?'

'Only a few minutes,' said Natalya, allowing Kat to concentrate. 'Though this does depend on how much information Kat is trying to download and if she has any security systems to bypass. And then, of course, she will be uploading a virus to scramble the whole system.'

The team waited in silence as Kat did her thing. Ethan was impressed; she was completely focused on what she was doing and looked amazingly calm.

'Done!'

Ethan and the rest looked over to see Kat stowing her portable hard drive in a pocket.

'Then let's get out quick,' said Ethan. 'I don't like the fact we're leaving anyone in this place while we skip out on a helicopter. But at least if we get out fast then the rescue op can be initiated, right?'

'Absolutely,' said Luke. 'And don't worry, Ethan; Gabe and Sam have things sorted. This place is as good as dead already and everyone is going to be safe within the hour. OK?'

'I guess,' said Ethan. Luke was right, he knew that, but it was still difficult for him to forget all the boys below them in the fort. He knew what they were feeling, how their life had become little more than surviving day to day with no hope of getting out. 'Come on, then,' he said, forcing himself to focus on the fact that the UKSF would be in only minutes after their exit, 'let's get shifting.'

Still lost in his thoughts, Ethan opened the door. He found himself face-to-face with one of the instructors.

The man didn't exactly look pleased to see him.

27

'You!'

Ethan froze: it was the instructor he'd taken down in the shower block during his escape and, despite his own face being broken up with streaks of black paint, the bloke still obviously recognized him. *Crap.*

Confusion was written across the instructor's face. And that moment of hesitation, Ethan knew, was his downfall: Natalya sprang forward, past Ethan, and slammed into the instructor. He had no time to react, respond or cry out. A blur of movement and he dropped to the floor, close to unconscious. Luke had him gagged and tagged before he had a chance to recover. Natalya, Ethan saw, wasn't even out of breath.

'He wasn't expecting to see you, was he?' said Natalya, and Ethan was sure he saw a flicker of a smirk on her usually calm face. 'Particularly as you are supposed to be dead.'

An alarm sounded.

'Bollocks!'

'Fair point, Eth,' said Johnny.

'But how did he sound an alarm?' asked Kat, stepping forward. 'He's alone and Natalya had him out of the game before he'd had a chance to even register what was going on.'

The sound of a door slipping shut cracked the conversation like a smashed bottle.

'There!' hissed Luke, pointing further on down the corridor to the door Ethan knew led to the rest of the facility. 'We've been pinged!'

'I think he came from the staff room,' said Ethan. 'Reckon there's anyone else in there?'

'If there was,' said Luke, 'then I would guess it was them who set the alarm and bolted.' He turned to Kat. 'We need to get a move on. Whoever that alarm's called, I'm not exactly in a hurry to meet them.'

Suddenly Johnny called from a far corner of the room where he was pointing at a computer screen, showing what looked like CCTV footage.

'Where's this, Eth? You didn't mention a dock.'

Ethan jogged over and saw on the screen a man in a vaulted space, obviously in the very bowels of the structure. It had a small stone landing, attached to which was a serious-looking power boat sat in inky sea water.

'That's because I've never seen it before.' Then Ethan recognized the man on the screen. 'That's the bastard who runs this place: Chief. The ex-Israeli special forces guy Sam mentioned right at the start, remember? What's he doing?'

'Escaping, by the look of it,' said Johnny. 'And that's not really playing fair, is it?'

'No,' said Ethan. 'I mean, what he's actually doing right this minute. Look – he's fiddling with something. Looks like a large box or container. What is it?'

They both knew exactly what it was, but it took Kat, who'd dashed over to see what they were looking at, to say it.

'Oh, God, that's a bomb. This place is rigged to blow!'

'That is not all,' said Natalya. 'Look here also.'

The team turned as one and there, on a screen, was the cage. Two boys were inside it and both were on the floor, one kneeling, the other flat out, trying to push himself back to his feet. Ethan recognized the boy lying on the floor immediately.

'Shit – it's Rick.'

Luke tried to hurry everyone along. 'Sam will be expecting us up top any minute. We need to move!'

Ethan felt his stomach churn; if Rick didn't get to his feet and the fight was judged to be over, he'd suffer the same fate as the one Ethan had been in the cage with himself. The thought of it sent him cold.

'I'm not leaving Rick to get murdered,' said Ethan.

'And we can't walk away from that either,' said Kat, looking at the image of the bomb on the screen.

'Gabe won't be pleased,' said Luke. 'It's seriously off mission.'

Kat flared at this. 'Are you suggesting we just let this place blow? There's probably enough explosive not just to damage this place, but to blow it sky-high!'

'She's right,' said Johnny. 'That thing goes off, it'll kill everyone.'

Luke turned to Ethan. 'Well, where is it, then? Ethan, you said you'd never seen that place before.'

'No, I haven't,' said Ethan. 'But it must be right in the depths of this place. I've never seen a door for it though.' Then he had a hunch. 'The cage!'

'What about it?' asked Johnny.

'I forgot,' said Ethan. 'There's a door the other side of the cage room. I bet that leads down there; it'd be an easy way to dispose of the loser's body, wouldn't it?'

'Makes sense,' said Luke.

Ethan didn't wait for any further discussion. He headed to the door and was back out in the hall, going back the way they'd come in. The team were on his heels.

'It's that door there,' he said with a nod. 'The one on the left.' But as he reached it, he hesitated.

'You OK, Eth?' asked Johnny.

Ethan nodded. 'I swore I'd never go back in here,' he said.

'I'll go first,' Johnny offered.

Ethan didn't give him a chance and slammed a boot into the lock. The door burst inwards and Ethan charged through, not thinking about what was on the other side. He knew only that every extra second he wasted was another second closer to this place going sky-high and all those down below being wiped out.

The place was dark, but spotlights were on and the sound of cameras took Ethan right back to his fight. He shook the memory from his mind, saw the cage and caught sight of another door in the wall behind it. Then, as he made to go to the cage, two instructors appeared out of the darkness like a picture coming into focus. Gabe, thought Ethan, had been on the nail about the additional security.

Using the full weight of his body at speed, Ethan rammed into them. Neither had time to dodge and were sent stumbling backwards. Johnny was on one before he could respond. Ethan heard the instructor drop to the floor with a moan, but didn't look to see what Johnny had done; the other instructor was getting to his feet. Ethan was into him before he had a chance to react, launching a kick at his stomach. The instructor took the blow like a pro, and came back at Ethan, who found himself suddenly on the ground, looking into the eyes of a man who was about to pummel him senseless. Ethan blocked a barrage of punches then got lucky with a return punch under the instructor's chin; it crunched his jaw together and Ethan knew he'd broken some teeth. With a twist of his hips, Ethan managed to flip the instructor off and onto his side, but before he landed, he grabbed his shirt and nutted him one. The instructor's nose exploded and he fell to the floor, dazed and confused and bleeding.

Ethan, relieved, saw Johnny nod at him.

'I'll tag them,' said Johnny, 'you sort the lads in the cage.' Johnny then looked back to Luke and the two girls. 'You lot, head across to the door opposite and get to that bomb! I'm in no mood to be blown up.'

As Johnny grabbed some plastic ties from a pocket, Ethan and the rest of the team did exactly as he had said. Ethan saw them dash past the cage to the other door, pulling it behind them. He then turned his attention to the cage, made to head over, but a movement caught his eye. It was another instructor, who'd obviously kept himself hidden in the shadows and was making to sneak out.

Two things then happened. One, Ethan saw that the man was carrying a pistol; he knew it would have been used to dispatch the loser of the fight, in this case, Rick, but he'd obviously been disturbed by the alarm. And two, the man realized Ethan had seen him.

The instructor stopped, went to draw his weapon.

In normal circumstances, Ethan would've got the hell out of the way. But this was different. He closed the gap. By the time the weapon was at the ready, Ethan was close enough to deal with it, grabbing it with his left hand and driving the pistol down into the stomach of the instructor. It was a drill he'd done dozens of times with Natalya, and he went through it like clockwork. Before the instructor was able to react to what was happening, he had a broken nose, his pistol had been snatched from his hand, snapping a finger in the process, and he was on the floor.

Ethan was now holding the pistol. It felt heavy in his hand. Solid and deadly. But he'd never used a pistol in his life. And wasn't about to start now. He tossed it behind him and into the dark.

The instructor was dazed and was trying to use his head to give himself enough leverage to stand. It was doing no good at all and Johnny, slipping past Ethan, tagged his hands and feet.

'Grab his jacket first,' said Ethan. 'Those two in the cage need it more than he does.'

Taking the jacket, Ethan headed over to the cage. The door was open; they really had got there just in time, he thought, looking back at the instructor who'd had the pistol. Just a minute more and he'd have been in the cage to use the weapon on Rick and finish him off for good. He climbed in. Johnny joined him.

'They alive?'

Ethan dropped to Rick's side. He was beginning to stir.

'Yeah,' he said, helping Rick sit up.

A voice cracked through on the chat-net. It was Luke.

'This isn't going quite according to plan. We're pinned down with gunfire!'

'Come on,' said Johnny, 'we gotta go. Now!'

Rick stared up at Ethan. His eyes were bloodshot and his face was nothing but a bruise. He could barely see through the tears streaming down his cheeks.

'Don't . . . kill me . . . please . . .' he stuttered.

Another call came through from Luke. 'We need some help here, guys. Move it!'

Ethan could feel Rick shivering and he knew it was from fear as much as the cold, plus the adrenaline from the fight.

'I'm not going to kill you,' he said. 'You're safe now. Nothing else will happen to you, I promise.'

'But those men . . . they made us fight. Told us they'd shoot us if we didn't.'

'You don't need to worry now,' said Ethan, thankful that even though that instructor had recognized him, Rick was still too much in shock from what he'd experienced to register just who was in front of him now. 'Someone will be here soon to take you home.'

'I want to go home now,' said Rick, almost talking to

himself. 'I need to. I should never have walked out. Things got out of hand . . .'

'You will,' said Ethan, choking down the anger inside at what had been done, not just to Rick, but to all the boys who'd ended up here. 'You just need to wait here, OK? You'll be safe. Someone will come and get you. Do you understand?'

Rick nodded weakly.

Ethan looked at the one who'd obviously won the fight. 'You – go out through that door, go down a few doors and you'll find a staff room. There should be some coats and stuff hanging on the wall. Bring them back here and keep warm. Understand?'

The boy nodded and stumbled out of the cage.

Johnny turned to the other door to follow the rest of the team. 'So, Eth; who shall we rescue next?'

'Luke, I think,' said Ethan, following on behind. 'What was that about being pinned down?'

'We'll find out when we get there,' said Johnny. 'Come on!'

From the room with the cage, Ethan and Johnny found themselves running down a steep staircase, which ended at a short, wide corridor. In the far wall was a door. They both heard the gunfire coming from behind it before they arrived.

Johnny called through on the chat-net. 'The cavalry's here, people! Sit rep?'

'We're to the right of the door as you come in,' came Luke in reply. 'He's trying to get the boat moving and failing. And we can't move because he's got us pinned down.'

'Oh, so that's what all those bangs are,' said Johnny.

'Shut up and do something!' hissed Kat's voice, in place of Luke's.

'Flash-bangs?' said Johnny, with a wink at Ethan. 'The rest of you, heads down, eyes closed and cover your ears!'

Ethan nodded and pulled one from a black pouch attached to his belt. 'After three . . .'

28

'Three!'

Ethan burst through the door, saw the boat floating away from the jetty and lobbed the grenade at it. Then he hit the deck. The flash-bang landed on the boat before blasting out white light and an ear-bursting noise.

Ethan was on his feet and saw the instructor he'd been forced to call Chief. Though still armed, he was dazed from the flash-bang and was stumbling around the boat.

Remembering everything he'd gone through at the hands of this man and his minions, and what had just happened to Rick, Ethan charged forward. He leaped across the increasing expanse of water between the boat and the jetty and crashed into Chief, knocking the pistol from his hand to clatter across the boat deck and sending them both to the floor.

Ethan could hear the boat's engine ticking over and felt the sway of the craft in the water. He was suddenly back to when he'd met Rick, trapped in that suffocating darkness in the bottom of a boat, probably *this* same bloody boat, drenched in sea water and the stench of diesel.

Ethan pulled himself to his feet and saw that the boat was now too far away from the jetty for him to jump off. He made ready for an attack, but his legs were kicked from under him. As he landed on the deck, he saw Chief coming at him and rolled out of the way as a heavy boot came at his head like it was a football. He was on his feet and ready as another attack came, this time a flurry of punches that he managed to defend himself against with his forearms, more by instinct than anything else. A couple of punches made it through, cracking him in the mouth, drawing blood.

Ethan knew he was out of his depth. He wasn't just fighting an instructor, he was up against the one who probably trained them all in the first place.

A combination of kicks and punches came. Ethan side-stepped to his left and in the same motion drove in with a left jab. It caught Chief on his chin. But all it did was anger him rather than do any damage and once again Ethan was on the defensive, trying more to stay out of trouble than anything else.

Kat's voice came over the chat-net. 'Ethan, we've got a problem.'

'No shit!' yelled Ethan as a punch narrowly missed crushing his windpipe into his spine. But he knew Kat couldn't hear him – he was in no position to squeeze the throat mics to communicate with the rest of the team, and the sound of the engine would have drowned out his voice.

'We can't do anything with the bomb. The only way to disarm it is with a key. And I'll bet you can guess who has it.'

Ethan barely had time to register what Kat had said when a sharp kick caught him in the stomach, winding him and sending him down coughing and spluttering like an engine refusing to start. He pushed himself to his feet again; he knew getting caught on the floor would be the end of him.

The next thing he felt was a sharp jab in his back that made him snap up straight.

'Who are you?'

Ethan said nothing. Another jab in his back. He stole a look over his shoulder to see that Chief was now back in possession of the pistol and had it in his right hand. Ethan calmed himself down. He had to get out of this. Natalya's training was about to get a serious testing.

'I asked you a question – where is your tongue?'

Another jab.

With a twist clockwise, Ethan whipped round to bring his chest up against the outside of Chief's right arm. He gripped it hard against his own chest, and then punched hard. He could feel Chief struggling against the grip he had on the arm holding the pistol, but he was unable to do anything as Ethan refused to stop his attack. He saw blood, but that just drove him on and he landed more punches.

Chief was yelling, his arm falling weak now, unable to hold up against the attack.

Ethan switched to the pistol and broke it out of Chief's hand. The sheer violence of the movement not only broke

Chief's finger, but wrenched his arm round so quickly that he had no choice but to follow it. He landed on the ground, cracking the side of his head hard on the boat deck. The movement also caused Ethan to lose hold of the pistol. Before he had a chance to recover, it slipped from his hands and bounced out of the boat into the water below.

Ethan heard Chief getting to his feet. He didn't look in great shape; his right eye was swollen shut, his ear mashed and cuts and bruises covered his face and neck. Ethan could hardly believe he'd done so much damage so quickly, or that Chief was up and coming back for more.

'You fight well,' said Chief, wiping the blood from his face. 'Guts and instinct and every defence into an attack. *Krav Maga*, yes?'

Ethan didn't reply; he'd spotted something on the boat deck just where Chief had landed. It was a key on the end of a chain, and seeing as the boat engine was running, he guessed it had to be the one for the bomb.

'Ethan!' came Kat's voice, sounding more desperate, 'If this timer's correct, we've only got five minutes before this thing goes off. And we really don't want to be here for that, OK?'

Ethan squeezed his throat mic. 'I'm doing the best I can!'

The next voice to come on the chat-net was calm and cool. 'Ethan. It is Natalya. You can beat him. He is more experienced, yes, but you just need to use what he throws at you against him, yes? You have the element of surprise; he does not know how skilled you are. Now finish it.'

Yes he does, thought Ethan. *He's just gone and bloody well guessed it . . .*

As if on cue, Chief attacked, first with a flash of punches, then a kick aimed at Ethan's knee. Ethan saw it coming and allowed his knee to crumple as it connected, sending him to roll across the floor towards the key. But as his fingers went to slip around it, Chief got there first, hoofing Ethan across the deck of the boat like a rugby ball, before picking up the key and slipping the chain over his head.

Coughing, exhausted, Ethan gripped the side of the boat and pulled himself back onto his feet. His muscles were burning and his legs felt as though they were about to collapse like wet straws. And his reactions were slowing.

Chief came in again, and even though Ethan got his hands up to protect his face and the side of his head, a left-hand hook caught him hard and dropped him to the floor. Ethan felt like he'd been slammed by a tree; he could see bright stars twinkling in front of him. He tried to get up, hadn't the energy, fell back down.

Chief approached and Ethan pushed himself away, slipping across the boat deck.

'Do not run from the inevitable. You have fought well, so accept your fate like a true warrior. Come!'

Ethan felt a huge fist grip the top of his head and wrench at his hair, pulling him up to his feet. It felt like his scalp was being ripped off and he yelled out in pain.

Chief leaned in close, bending down next to Ethan's ear. 'I am afraid this might hurt a little . . .'

Ethan shot a look up at Chief and saw him raising his fist to bring it down into his face. And he knew that after that first blow knocked him senseless, Chief would finish him off for good. There would be no waking up.

Ethan dug deep for every last bit of energy he had left. Then, as Chief smiled in anticipation of the killing blow, Ethan launched his foot between Chief's legs. He wasn't sure about range or direction, he just hoped it was hard enough to have an effect.

It was. And it did.

Chief roared and Ethan felt his grip on his hair slacken. Taking the advantage, Ethan reached up and grabbed Chief's arm, bending the thumb in hard till it snapped like a chicken leg. As Chief roared even louder, Ethan went in with two kicks, then used the weight of his body to twist the arm. Chief went with it and toppled forward out of the boat with a yell.

As the heavy man tumbled towards the water, the chain round his neck swung in a wide arc. Somehow Ethan managed to catch hold of the key. He yanked hard. The chain snapped and Ethan had the key in his hand! He flung it onto the stone jetty, but in the process felt himself topple forward.

Coughing and spluttering, Ethan resurfaced in the water, but only in time to see Chief pull himself into the boat and at last get it moving. The darkness seemed to then suck him out of the dock through an arch in the wall and into the night.

'Ethan? Grab my arm!'

Sweat and sea water blinding him, Ethan thrashed out wildly to find the hand of whoever it was calling him. Panic caught hold as he felt his energy going and he knew he was about to slip under the water. Then he felt himself heaved up and onto the jetty, coughing and spluttering, his whole body screaming pain.

Ethan opened his eyes to see Kat smiling at him. 'You did

it,' she said. 'The bomb's out of action. Now all we need to do is get up top and call Sam in to pick us up. You able to stand?'

A few minutes later, having run out onto the top of the fortress, Ethan watched Sam bring the helicopter in. They'd all picked up their rigs and as soon as he'd touched down they clambered into the back. Sam took off immediately.

'Job done?'

'As always,' said Johnny, responding to Sam's voice on the chat-net. 'And with a not unsurprising dash of style and panache. You know, I sometimes think people get into crime just so that they can meet me.'

'The Regiment will be here in minutes. Well done, team. Job well done.'

Ethan, like the rest, squeezed his throat mic and said, 'Thanks,' but it was relief above all that he felt rather than pride. He was knackered, bruised and bloodied, and he'd barely got away with his life.

It was all he could do to stop himself crying.

29

'Drink?'

Ethan took the can from Johnny, who was standing next to him in the kitchen of the flat wearing a rubber face mask of President Kennedy. He snapped the ring pull, drank deep.

'I was going to ask if you wanted a glass, but I guess not.'

Ethan took it anyway, and emptied the can into it.

'How are you doing?'

'All right,' said Ethan, though he was still in agony every morning when he got out of bed. He'd spent the last few weeks either exercising or getting beaten up. It had certainly taken its toll.

It was only a week since the job had finished and he and the rest of the Raiders were all round at Johnny's flat, not just to celebrate Ethan's moving in, but also another completed mission.

It hadn't exactly gone smoothly. They'd got the intel for Gabe, and the UKSF had busted the place wide open, rescuing the boys still there. Ethan had heard as well that Rick had been sent back to his very relieved parents. But it wasn't a total success – and that bugged him. And as for his experience in the cage; he hadn't had a decent night's sleep since they'd returned. Nightmare images still woke him up in a cold sweat.

'You're a tough bastard, you know that?' said Johnny.

'I just didn't like the idea of dying,' said Ethan. 'I'm hardly Bruce Lee.'

'Pity,' said Johnny, 'because what we really need more than anything on this team is a ninja.'

Kat called through from the lounge. 'Johnny? Ethan? The film's about to start. It's Bodhi time!'

'Remind me why we're watching *Point Break*,' asked Ethan.

'Because it's one of the greatest action movies ever made. And it's my favourite film,' Johnny replied.

'Oh, that explains it then. And do you always dress as one of the characters for every movie you watch, or just this one?'

'Just this one!' said Johnny. 'And after *Point Break*, I've got *Roadhouse*, *Die Hard*, *Rambo 4* . . .'

'You're sick, you know that?'

'But happy, and that's what's important.'

Kat called them again.

'Come on,' said Johnny. 'Don't want to miss any of it, do we?'

'Guess not,' said Ethan and followed Johnny through to the lounge. He squeezed in between Kat and Natalya and took another chug from his glass.

'You look very serious,' said Kat. 'What's bothering you?'

'The same thing that should be bothering us all,' said Natalya. 'That it wasn't a clean job. That it wasn't as it should be? I am right, Ethan, yes?'

Ethan nodded. They were supposed to be covert operators, sneaky, but instead everything had kicked off big time. They'd bust the cage fighting, saved the lads and Gabe was more than happy with the intel they'd bagged from the server. But Mr X had escaped, as had the Chief, and that had pissed off everyone. Wherever they were, wherever they'd gone, no one had a clue. They were ghosts and that was bad.

Johnny stood up. 'I think we need a toast to get us going,' he said. 'On your feet.'

'Shut up, Johnny,' said Kat.

'No. Come on – up! We need this party more than anything and it's my job to ensure we all enjoy it. So we're not yet perfect. So the bad guys got away. There'll be another time. And we can now get back to practising for the competitions. In just a few months we'll be bringing medals home by the dozen!'

Ethan joined the rest in getting to his feet. It was good to hear the mention of the competitions. In the haze since coming back, he hadn't really given it much thought. He'd caught up with his mum and Jo, checked they were OK. And they were, not least because his dad had been arrested. They'd bought his story about being away practising and said how much they were looking forward to coming over and seeing him in the flat. It was all so normal, so everyday; and it was completely at odds with everything Ethan and the rest had just gone through. The idea of getting back into skydiving, focusing only on that, felt good. It was the kind of medicine that he knew for sure had a good chance of sorting him out and clearing his head.

'Right, everyone,' said Johnny slipping easily into the role of master of ceremonies, 'raise your glasses or cans or whatever it is you've got in your hands.'

As they all did so, Kat asked, 'What's the toast?'

'Actually I just want to do *this*.' Johnny whipped round to face Luke and snapped open his can. It exploded. Luke disappeared in a fountain of raging fizz. It drenched him in a second. As Luke stood there, doing a very good impression of a drowned spaniel, Johnny said, 'There, now doesn't that feel better? Everyone? Luke?'

Ethan couldn't help himself. With all that he'd gone through, seeing Luke utterly drenched seemed so completely ridiculous that he just burst out laughing.

'Thanks, Ethan,' said Luke. 'Nice to know that you care.'

'Here,' said Johnny, and handed Luke a fresh can.

Luke promptly emptied it all over Johnny. And at that laughter took over and the whole team collapsed back into their chairs, tears in their eyes.

As Johnny started the movie Ethan got up to go and get another drink. He made his way to the bathroom where the bath itself was filled with ice and cans. He was half tempted to jump in.

Pulling a can out, plus a few extras for everyone else, he headed back. As he went to sit down, Kat beamed at him and he realized it was a smile he could quite easily live with seeing again and again and again. There was nothing he could do to get away from it; she was stunning. He felt sure Sam wouldn't want them getting involved with each other in case it somehow jeopardized operations but he was beginning to wonder how to avoid the inevitable – or if he wanted to avoid it!

Kat said, 'You OK, Ethan?'

'What?'

'You look a bit dazed.'

Ethan did his best to recover and squeezed back in next to her on the sofa. 'No, I'm fine,' he said.

'You sure? What you went through; that was tough.'

Ethan nodded.

'If you need to talk about it . . .'

'No,' said Ethan. 'To be honest, tonight is exactly what I need.'

Kat once again sent one of her killer smiles his way. Ethan said no more and turned his attention to the movie; he had a feeling that if he said anything he'd make a tit of himself.

About half an hour into the film a very familiar engine growl pushed its way through an open window.

Johnny got up, walked over, pulled back a curtain. 'Sam.'

'He doesn't usually come to things like this,' said Kat. 'Normally keeps his distance from us. Probably afraid we'll see his softer side if he has a drink with us.'

A knock rapped at the door and Johnny answered it. Sam followed him back into the flat. Everyone nodded, no one said a word. Sam walked into the lounge and pulled out a folder.

Then Ethan asked the question on everyone's lips. 'What is it, Sam? What's going on?'

Sam stared at the team and gave a two-word answer: 'Party's over.'